THIS BRAVE BALANCE

Rusalka Reh

TRANSLATED BY KATY DERBYSHIRE

THIS BRAVE
BALANCE

To an incredible reader:
Gilberto Miron

amazoncrossing 🌐

Text copyright © 2011 by Rusalka Reh
English translation copyright © 2011 Amazon Content Services
LLC

This Brave Balance by Rusalka Reh was originally published in
2010 by Verlagsgruppe Oetinger as Asphaltspringer.
Translated from the German by Katy Derbyshire.
First published in English in 2011 by AmazonCrossing.

Lyrics to "Shadow Blues" by Laura Veirs reprinted by permission
of Freak Off the Leash Music.

Published by AmazonCrossing
P.O. Box 400818
Las Vegas, NV 89140

Library of Congress Control Number: 2010918617
ISBN-13: 978-1-61109-005-5
ISBN-10: 1611090059

TABLE OF CONTENTS

Many thanks to
"Parkour Leipzig"

"His gaze fell upon the top story of the building adjoining the quarry. Like a light flicking on, the casements of a window flew open, a human figure, faint and insubstantial at that distance and height, leaned far out abruptly, and stretched both arms out even further. Who was it? A friend? A good person? Someone who cared? Someone who wanted to help? Was it just one person? Was it everyone? (…) He raised his hands and spread all his fingers."

—Franz Kafka, *The Trial* (translated by Breon Mitchell)

NAME DAY

I guess I'm not what you'd call the storytelling type. And maybe this isn't even a story. You think for a long time that everything's kinda OK. Nothing happens, or nothing much exciting. Just life, you know. And then later you look back and all that quiet crap suddenly ties up like the threads of some sticky spiderweb.

Us, that's Skylark, Corone, Jay, and me, Dipper. Kittiwake's one of us too—she turned ten last fall and she's Corone's sister. She usually tagged along when we practiced at the stadium or in the park. She's funny—how can I put it? She's not quite all there, but she was born that way, says Corone, and it's no reason to treat her mean. And nobody does, 'cause Kittiwake's just fine and dandy.

It was Jay who brought the book along, when we were crashed out on the mattresses in the old exhibition hall. The rain was hissing down in streams, drumming on the metal roof and against the windows. We couldn't practice outside. Saut de détente on wet ground? Too dangerous. We'd been meeting up for parkour training since the spring. Every day. Our muscles had gradually gotten used to the extreme movements. We got a kick out of the way it got better and better for all of us. But we had to stick with it. Especially me, 'cause I had bit of a loser thing going on. To put it mildly.

Jay slung his backpack down next to the mattresses and himself on top of them. We all wobbled like Jell-o.

"Hey!" Skylark held his hand out to him. "Great weather, huh?"

Jay pulled his soaking wet sweatshirt over his head.

"The weather is not a constant and therefore not worth talking about." He gave Skylark five and they touched fists.

Typical Jay. He talked strange like that. I could swear he never once said the word "cool," right up to the last day I ever saw him. You wanna try that sometime.

He grabbed his backpack and rummaged around inside it. In the end he pulled out the book, the size of a postcard, in a brown cover spattered with grease spots.

"What's that?" Corone sat up, a bona fide bed-head look going on.

"*The Observer's Book of Birds.*" Jay opened it up.

"Are you switching from parkour to bird-watching?" asked Skylark.

We laughed. I heard a pigeon beating its wings beneath the roof of the hall.

"We're gonna choose new names for ourselves," said Jay, not bothered by our comments. "This book has the best names in it, perfect for parkour."

He threw the book down on the mattress right between us.

It was an awesome idea. We knew it right away.

Skylark opened the book and sneezed.

"Jeez, where'd you dig this thing up?"

"My mother left it behind," said Jay. "I guess she got it from a used bookstore."

Jay's parents were university dudes. Their whole place full of books and all that. Jay's mother had been living some- where else with his younger brother for a couple years, not sure where exactly, but anyway she didn't get on with the professor of miserable old law anymore. They hadn't been in contact since, Jay and his mother, pretty weird family shit. Not like the rest of us were much better. Take my mother— she's a restroom attendant at the Mercado mall. Has been for years. You wanna try that sometime.

So as Skylark flicked through this odd book we heard him mumbling, "Black-throated diver... Great Northern diver... Red-necked grebe... cormorant... spoonbill..."

"If we give ourselves new names we'll be free!" Jay jumped up all of a sudden. Something about him was different that day. His voice was trembling, and that was strange enough as it was. "It's like that in all the stories: if you know someone's name you have power over them. How many years have we been running around with the same names? And how many people have power over us? Hundreds? Thousands? It's time to reinvent ourselves!" He dropped down next to us again. Corone grunted—that meant something like approval from him. "And apart from that I had this dream," Jay said. "I was a bird, just floating, and it was so absolutely awesome. Parkour comes pretty close to that feeling, if you ask me. That's why I had the idea with the birds' names."

"I know all about birds," Corone said with a grin. He handed the book on to me. It had a bad stench of basement to it. "I had a real hot chick just last night."

Skylark fell on his back laughing.

"And being with an awesome chick," Corone added in an important tone, "comes pretty close to parkour as well."

Corone could be a real asshole. Just because he got all the girls he couldn't stop bragging, like he'd invented the Big Bang or something.

"Allow me to introduce myself." He got up and took a bow. "From now on you can call me Corone."

Jay smiled. "Hey, Corone. Welcome to the Urban Planetbirds."

We all got our new names that rainy day in the old exhibition hall. One day later, Corone's little sis started grouching that she wanted one too of course, and we christened her Kittiwake. I liked Dipper best. "Rather quick and quiet in its ways," the book said about dippers, and that was what we all wanted as traceurs: to get from A to B as fast and as smoothly as possible.

Jay was right. Parkour is kinda like flying. It makes you free because you leap over everything that gets in your way: fences, walls, trashcans, even garages if you like, anything and everything. You don't take detours. You don't let anything stop you. You're so totally absorbed in your body, you switch your head to empty and at the same time focus on everything, yeah, everything, and then you know. You know what's coming next. You react to every little thing that comes your way. And then: passement.

Jay explained it once like this: "You have to keep it clear in your mind: emptiness and at the same time anything's possible. Then you just run and everything you do is just right now and right now and now again."

He told me once that he was gonna be out of here someday.

"I'm going to disappear when Professor Bigshot gets too much for me. One day it'll be the last straw."

And Jay doesn't say that kind of thing for no reason. But back then I still didn't think there'd really be a last straw, because he could take a whole lot.

4

Professor Bigshot was his dad. They had this weird thing going. Either they avoided each other like the plague or they spent the whole time fighting like cats and dogs. Jay pretty much lived in his bedroom and only came out when he had to. His dad put him under crazy pressure. No wonder his wife ran off—and took Jay's younger brother with her, everybody's darling, the perfect son, always polite and well-behaved and straight-As all the way. Jay was supposed to work like that too, but he was too intelligent for that kinda thing, let's say. He had too much new stuff going on up there, inside his skull. He'd have died of boredom. And parkour was really important for him, so he didn't completely flip out in the company of Professor Bigshot.

You're a traceur—you have to be awake, wide awake.

Seeing and hearing everything.

Out there in the city, on the train, everywhere and anywhere.

So you can react.

COLD

At the spot in the park where we always started our training, all the leaves on the ground were brown; yellow threads hung from the weeping willows and the river shimmered gray. Nasty yellow foam snaked past us, scum on the river like plastic jellyfish props for a B-movie. And then the fog. That fog settled over everything, as if the curtain was being drawn on the year: a round of applause and it's all over.

I arrived late because my boss hadn't let me go. It was freezing cold. We all breathed out white clouds.

"Are you warmed up?" Jay called out to me.

I nodded. "I jogged all the way."

He took a run up, jumped, flew over the low wall on the side of the stairs in a squat, and pushed himself off with his hands at the last moment. He landed on soft feet, hardly making a sound.

"You're up now, Corone!" Jay jogged back to us as Corone took his run-up, levered himself sideways over the wall, and made a 360-degree turn on the way. He flew over the obstacle at the speed of light, landed totally controlled, and threw his arms up in the air.

"Woah! Awesome!" we shouted.

"We're training the saut de chat, man," said an annoyed Jay. "Ever heard of it? Why the révers?"

Corone strolled back to us, extra-slow. "Who are you, the sergeant major?" He looked Jay right in the eye. "I'm just a whole lot further along than you guys with your chat! You wanna turn up the speed a bit, dude!"

"So how's your new babe?" I asked Corone quickly, noticing Jay and he would be fighting again any minute—and that was too much stress. They were constantly bitching each other out.

Luckily, Corone took the bait. He swung himself onto the wall and lit a cigarette in a squat.

"I hardly see her anymore, I'm always here." He narrowed his eyes, blew his smoke upward. "She's started complaining real bad. Pretty annoying."

"Why don't you bring her along sometime? We never have enough girls here anyway." Jay squatted down alongside him. He took the cigarette out of his hand and took a drag on it. He didn't really smoke; it was more like smoking the peace pipe, a peace cigarette, that kinda thing.

"Maybe." Corone jumped soundlessly down from the wall. "Come on, guys. This is first-grade stuff."

Our next training location: the old part of the stadium grounds. An endless lawn with sixty-foot floodlights, a gravel path and trees and then a yellow building with a tower. Stairs leading up to it, three hundred feet wide at least. At the bottom two porta-potties. Cuddling up like a couple in love, or that's what Kittiwake says. At the top of the stairs: flagpoles, rails, walls. Shrill voices and screams wafted over to us from the fall fairground next to the stadium.

"Oh nooo!" shouted Skylark.

He'd run up the stairs ahead of us and tested out a jump against the wall. Saut de bras.

"What's up?" called Jay.

"They got rid of the graffiti. Now it's totally slippery," said Skylark as we ran up to him, taking each step separately—that was part of our power training.

"Pretty subpar, you're right," pronounced Jay once he'd tried it too. "We can still practice, but keep it modest, guys. There are sand-blasted walls everywhere, there's not much we can do about it."

We hadn't been training for ten minutes when we heard a huge commotion.

"Gimme that!" The voice was even shriller than the fairground soundtrack. "I wanna go, gimme it!"

We ran along the wall to the edge. I came to a stop behind Jay, Corone rammed into my back, and I slammed against Jay. He swayed, falling forward. I tried to grab him but it all went too fast. As he fell I thought—that's it, something had to give. Now it's payday. A twenty-five-foot drop and your brain's meatloaf. But Jay twisted round in midair like a flash and grabbed hold of the edge of the wall with both hands a second later.

"Shit!" screamed Skylark.

"Jaaayyy!" That was Kittiwake.

With a clatter she dropped the iPod she'd just taken away from a boy, and ran to the wall.

"Watch out, watch out!" she yelled. "Kittiwake's gonna catch Jay!"

She stretched out her arms.

"Get out the way!" gasped Jay, but Kittiwake stayed right where she was.

Jay moved away from her slowly, hand over hand, stopping above the porta-potties. He dangled about twenty feet above them. There was a grid on the wall below him, and he somehow managed to jump onto it and lower himself downward bit by bit. At last he landed on one of the roofs.

I gave a deep breath of relief, like you wouldn't believe.

"But that toilet you're on is for ladies," said an amazed Kittiwake, trotting over to Jay.

He jumped onto the gravel path right before her feet. "How do you know?" he asked her with a smile.

Kittiwake pointed at a handwritten sign on one of the doors.

"Lay-dees," she read.

"Hey, where did you learn to read?" Jay gave a whistle through his teeth.

Kittiwake grinned. "Dipshit school!" she said proudly.

We all laughed like crazy, the two of them down there and us on top of the wall, even though it wasn't even a joke. Kittiwake really did go to a school for dipshits, it was the truth and nothing but the truth. We were just laughing because everything had turned out OK.

"That's my toilet," explained Kittiwake seriously, "because girls are ladies. The one next to it is yours."

Skylark called out: "But Jay's not a gentleman, Kittiwake!"

"What is he then?" asked Kittiwake.

"Anyone ever told you you're a freak?" shouted Skylark.

The monster wall next to the staircase outside the stadium is almost twelve feet high, and it's the grand finale of every training session. None of us loves that wall—it's a real challenge. Right at the beginning, Jay fell off it once and dislocated his shoulder.

Skylark took a run-up, tried to grab the edge, and slipped down.

"Don't run into the wall," said Jay. "Push off upwards for passe muraille!"

He made it the next time and pulled himself up.

"Freezing cold, dudes!" he called out.

"Then move your ass!" growled Corone. "Or get yourself pocket warmers!"

I was up next. It was just so odd to run up against that huge wall at full speed. I gave up after my fifth try. I'd never get it right. Jeez, I was such a loser.

Skylark came down the stairs, holding out his bright red hands. His palms were bleeding in a couple places.

"I'm outta here," he said. "It's too cold for me. I'm getting all cut up." He grabbed his backpack and slung on his hip bag.

"Yella," Corone taunted him.

"You leaving already?" Jay asked, surprised. And as Skylark blew a white cloud in his face, Jay said: "It's not going to get any warmer, you know. Does that mean you're giving up till spring?"

Skylark sat down on the steps, annoyed, Corone next to him, me leaning against the ice-cold metal rail. Kittiwake started searching through a fancy glittery red purse she had; it was new. Jay paced up and down in front of us.

"Let's go to my place and think about what to do in winter," he said in the end.

We got up. Only Kittiwake hadn't heard what Jay had said. Absolutely concentrated, she was squatting on the cold stairs and looking at this funny gray brochure. There was a church on the front, and when I looked over her shoulder I saw photos of organs. No kidding. Church organs. Kittiwake was funny like that. You never knew what was going on up there.

"Let's go, Kittiwake!" yelled Jay. "You've never been to my house, have you? Come on!"

She leapt up and ran after us.

PROFESSOR BIGSHOT

"Ah, the would-be stuntmen! How's things, how's school going?"

Jay's father was sitting on a white leather armchair in the living room, a metal floor lamp lighting up a magazine on his lap. As he said hello he closed the pages and shoved the mag under his seat. He came toward us with a smile, gave Skylark his hand and laid the other on his arm, then he shook mine and boxed me on the shoulder as if we were old buddies.

"And who do we have here?" he asked, bending down to Kittiwake.

"That's my sister," said Corone.

"My name's Kittiwake," she said.

"Aha," said Professor Bigshot. "And what grade are you in?"

"Fourth grade."

"So you'll be starting at grammar school next year then, won't you?"

Grammar school. Oh boy.

"No, I'm staying at my school where I am now." Kitti-wake walked straight across the totally lavish room to the shelves of CDs. "Have you got any organ music?" she asked, her head slanting as if she was reading the titles.

12

Professor Bigshot gave a strange laugh and put a CD on for Kittiwake. We made the most of the opportunity and beat it upstairs to Jay's room.

"Take a seat," said Jay.

He knelt down at his record player, pulled Linkin Park out of the sleeve, put it on the turntable like a raw egg on a spoon, and lowered the needle to the groove. A krrrkrrrkrrr came out of the speakers before the first track kicked in. Sometimes I like that krrr at least as much as the music that comes next.

"It looks like we need a training hall for the winter," Jay started in. "How can we go about raising enough rent for, let's say, three afternoons a week? It only has to be for…" He added it up, gazing into a corner of the room where a cloth with some fat Asian dude on it was hung on the wall. "For about four months. What do you guys think?"

"Sure, it'll be OK again in April," said Skylark. "But I really don't know how we can get the money together. We all have school or a job, parkour training, then homework…"

"Exactly," I butted in, seeing my last few free minutes going down the drain. "D'you want us to start flipping patties at Burger King, or what?"

"Hey, Comrade Dipper, d'you want to support even more cows making the hole in the ozone layer even bigger with their farts?" Skylark always launched straight into political lectures. He could really kill you like that sometimes. "Maybe we could get rid of some of our private stuff," he thought out loud. "Haven't you guys got something we could sell off? A CD player, or a pile of silk socks with comfort elastic?"

It was all right for him. His parents had money and all that.

"I'm not gonna steal nothing," I said quickly. "My ma'd go gray overnight if she found out. I can't do that to her."

"Relax, dude," said Corone. "Who said anything about stealing? We wanna train and not end up in jail. I'm guessing the parkour obstacles in a prison cell get pretty dull in the long run. And you really need the training, Dipper. Otherwise you won't get your ass over the monster wall even in a year's time."

I didn't reply.

Jay was lying on the carpet, hands behind his head, staring at the ceiling. Linkin Park was creating a weird mix with the organ music from downstairs.

The door opened and Kittiwake came in.

"Jay's pa put on organ music for me!" She fetched two handfuls of walnuts out of her sweatshirt pocket and arranged them in a heart shape on the carpet. "And he gave me nuts, too!"

Jay swung himself upright. "As long as none of us have an efficient idea that will really get us money and not a jail sentence, we'll just have to keep training outside," he said, summing up our admittedly pathetic discussion.

"What do you need money for?" asked Kittiwake, messing up the heart.

"For a training hall so we don't freeze to death, you know?" answered Jay, and his voice was real gentle, as if Kittiwake was an angel and he might frighten her if he spoke normally.

Kittiwake put a nut between her teeth and bit down on the shell. Everyone pulled a face at the cracking sound. She spat out the two halves into her hands, jumped up, and disappeared downstairs again.

"Crazy shit: suddenly she loves organ music," said Corone. "Isn't that a bit much for a kid from the dipshit school?"

"Hey, come on," said Jay. "Music's something primeval. It gets to everyone, never mind all that questionable IQ stuff."

"Music, OK, but organ music? You ever heard that droning shit? No, whatever you say, I can't get my brain round it!" Corone shook his head.

"Well my dad'll certainly be pleased to have a new friend to listen to Bach's organ concertos with," laughed Jay.

"So," Skylark interrupted, "let's get back to the subject." He took a slice of pizza off a plate next to Jay's bed and bit into it. I mean, no kidding, I could *hear* that pizza had been lying there for exactly six days, thirteen hours, eight minutes, and thirty-three seconds. You wanna try biting into something like that.

Chewing, he said: "The thing with the hall's out of our league, I guess. We'll just carry on like before, OK? Stay independent. And no more moaning and groaning from me—I promise."

"Word!" said Corone, and gave Skylark a high five.

Skylark was right, even if he was eating that ancient piece of pizza. I was cold outside too, but you can bet David Belle's father never broke his head over the bad weather in Germany when he was in Vietnam.

The door opened again.

"My God, it looks like someone dropped a bomb in here!" Professor Bigshot looked around, disgusted. "You could call up Shell and ask if they want to store their spilled oil in here. It would hardly make any difference."

15

Kittiwake came into the room as well and beamed up at him. A clear case of organ music bribery, I thought.

"This young lady's just been telling me about your plans."

He was wearing slacks, in beige, with a belt pretty high up.

"You need money to rent a hall, did I get that right? The young lady was slightly excited when she told me."

He put one hand on Kittiwake's shoulder.

"We were thinking about it, yes," said a suspicious Jay.

"I thought I might be able to help you out." His father stuck his hands quickly in his beige pants pockets, and I thought of weasels disappearing into holes in the sand. "Not without something in return, of course." He paused for a moment. "I'll pay the rent for a hall. And you guys do jobs around the house, whatever comes up. Your mother's room needs clearing out. The garden has to be got ready for winter. Et cetera, et cetera."

"I can help you too, can't I?" asked Kittiwake, gazing at Professor Bigshot as if he was Leonardo DiCaprio, at least.

"But of course you can help me," he said loudly, as if there was something up with her ears. "We can put all the CDs in the right order and listen to Bach while we do it. Hm?"

"No." Jay was standing up now. Facing his father. The word dangled between their heads like in neon letters.

"No?" asked Professor Bigshot, irritated.

"We don't need a hall. We'll carry on training outside."

His father took his weaselly hands out of his sandy pockets and knocked out a slow rhythm against the wardrobe next to the door. No idea what that was supposed to mean.

His pants were hanging off him, only held in place by his thin, mustard-yellow belt.

"Well, fine. You know best. It's certainly cold out, but I suppose that'll toughen you up. I only wanted to help."

"Can I still come round here again?" asked Kittiwake. She pouted.

"Of course you can," said Professor Bigshot.

He turned on his heel. As he left the room he asked, in that kind of voice that pretends nothing's up: "How did your math test go, Sebastian?"

"C-plus," was Jay's quiet answer.

"That's not good enough," said his father. It sounded sharp all of a sudden. "Come and see me downstairs when you've said goodbye to your friends."

Oh boy. If I'd have come home with a C+ for math, my mother woulda bought me a cake out of three days' worth of penny tips at the Mercado restrooms, with "Congratulations, Dipper!" in blue frosting on the top. I'd never gotten more than a D.

We weren't happy to leave Jay alone that evening.

"See ya tomorrow."

"Stay cool."

"So can I come back tomorrow?" asked Kittiwake, concerned now.

"Come on, let's go," Corone said and shoved her out the front door.

"Sure you can," said Jay with a smile, closing the door between us.

A KITE IS A BIRD

During school vacation, I usually got a job on a construction site so my ma could have a couple hours off. After school finished I just ended up staying there. I bought my ma an electric heating pad 'cause she always has trouble with her back, and she was happy as shit. Plus I have to buy myself new sneakers pretty often 'cause I go though them like crazy doing parkour. But luckily it doesn't matter if they're brand-name shoes or ten-dollar sneakers, so long as you feel good in them. The most important thing about your clothes is that they're comfortable, leaving you enough room to maneuver but not getting in the way of your movements.

Corone's mother did piece-work, packing ice in a factory in shifts. The fact is, there was an agreement between Corone and my ma—Kittiwake could go to my ma when there was nothing else doing. To the restroom paradise, I mean. My ma and her workmate Olga played board games with her. Kittiwake sat on a chair in the cubicle where they store the toilet paper, and spread out the board on top of the soap canisters. She took her move and then waited for my ma or Olga to come rushing in and make their move between wiping down toilet seats. No one was allowed to know there was a little girl sitting in there for hours on end, even if they are the cleanest toilets in the country by a long shot (thanks to my ma). All in all, it's not quite the right

18

location for a kid. Because when it comes down to it, people only go there to pee and crap. That's a fact. Unfortunately, that's what the lady from Child Protective Services thought too, when she came rushing into the restroom paradise one long Saturday when Ma had to work till midnight. She threatened to report my ma if she ever saw Kittiwake in there again. So that was the end of Kittiwake's board games in the restroom paradise, and we had her tagging along at our training sessions again. It was pretty annoying because it meant we couldn't always concentrate, and we made more mistakes because she was constantly talking or asking for something.

Corone didn't have a dad and Kittiwake didn't either, they'd "got lost along the way," Corone said, but that was all he was telling. I think that was why Kittiwake was so into Professor Bigshot, because she'd have liked to have a dad.

My father didn't run off; he died back when I was six. I guess he was a pretty good guy, my father, I really lucked out with him. But you don't stand a chance in hell against cancer, no matter how good a dad you are.

OK.

I hope it's not totally nerdy if I just happen to mention that I really wanted a girlfriend last fall. I mean, who doesn't? Everybody wants somebody. You can put on some big show and act like you're the coolest guy in the world, whatever—everyone wants a girlfriend.

So it was just too dumb that no girls ever came to training. Not one single girl all year long. Even though we had a site on the net with the times and places of our training sessions. There are traceuses all over the world now—they all put their videos online and I watch them, in the world's greatest flow. But they're all girls from Madrid or Munich or Helsinki, I don't know. Certainly farther away than would be convenient for me personally.

Like I said, I was sixteen last fall and I'd never had a girlfriend. So there's no need to add that I'd never slept with a girl. Boy, it goes round and round in your head. What it'd be like. If the others have ever done it. If you'd mess everything up. I thought about it pretty much all the time, and it drove me especially crazy when Corone pointed out for the hundredth time that he was having sex yesterday, today, and tomorrow. Boy, did that ever get on my nerves.

A couple of days later, Corone was suddenly in a pretty evil mood.

First I thought it was because he had Kittiwake in tow again, but that wasn't it. He didn't move his ass off the wall while the rest of us warmed up. Smoking his third cigarette in a row.

"Hey, Comrade Corone, something up?" Skylark was sitting on the wall in the splits.

"No," griped Corone. "Nothing up."

I was doing squat jumps onto the wall and off again. "Stress with Kittiwake?" I asked.

"No, for God's sake." Corone pressed out his cigarette. Rolled himself another one. Lit it up.

"Then warm up with us, come on," said Jay, rotating his arms. "You can't train if you're not warmed up."

Corone jumped off the wall and shoved at Jay with both hands. "You dumb shit!"

Jay stumbled two steps backward, but he got his balance again.

Corone yelled, "Just leave me alone for a minute, can't you? What makes you think you can boss me around? You sound like Professor Bigshot!"

It was scary. Like I said, Corone and Jay often argued, but neither of them had ever laid a hand on each other before.

Jay didn't fight back.

"OK, respect. I just don't want anything to happen to anyone," he said in a calm voice.

"You're not my freakin' father and you're certainly not my mother!"

Corone sat down again. Kittiwake went over and stroked his arm.

"Don't be mad," she said.

"I'm not mad! Leave me alone!"

It all seemed kinda unreal, like on a stage or something. The sun squished through a fat yellowy-gray layer of clouds in the sky; it was enough to make you feel sorry for it. A woman with a dog walked past down on the grass. Her jacket was so bright red I thought I had a filter over my pupils.

"Corone and Kite were in love," said Kittiwake, sweeping cigarette packs and dry leaves out of a corner of the wall with a long twig. "And now she's crying. Right, Corone?"

"Shut up!"

I started realizing he might just be having problems with his girlfriend.

"Kite? Who's Kite?" asked Skylark.

"Hey," said a voice behind my back.

I turned round.

"Kite, cool!" Kittiwake threw away her branch, running up to a girl I'd never seen before and almost crushing her.

"Jeez, what are you doing here?" Corone's cigarette drooped from the corner of his mouth as if it was attached to his lips.

"Just wanted to see what you guys get up to here."

"It's none of your business what we get up to." Corone swung round on top of the wall and stared out over the grass toward the river.

Wow, I thought. He's hardly said anything, but suddenly you can cut the air with a knife, it's so greasy, ice-cold, and dark.

"Hi, I'm Jay." Jay shook Kite's hand.

"Hey," she said again, and smiled like she'd made a huge mistake and only just noticed.

"Skylark." Shake, shake.

I had to dry my hand on my pants, the air was so greasy. That kinda thing always gets me real nervous. At some point it was fairly presentable again—my hand, I mean.

"Dipper." Shake.

"Do you want to join in?" Jay looked Kite up and down.

She was wearing sports gear, tight-fitting, which suited her pretty much down to a T. To put it mildly.

"If you don't mind." She squinted over at Corone, who still had his back to us as if he'd never seen anything as incredibly fascinating as the grass and the soccer players.

"Sure," said Skylark. "We're just warming up, OK?"

Corone squatted there like a statue on a plinth, and if it hadn't been for the blue clouds coming out of his mouth and nose every now and then, I wouldn't have known he was alive.

Kite was at least as supple as Skylark. I looked over at her furtively.

"Glad you've come along," said Jay.

"I wanted to come and train a couple of weeks ago," she explained as she did a few side stretches. "There was a parkour crew near where I lived in Wales. That's where I first saw it."

Behind her on the grass, someone was flying a kite. Kite, I thought suddenly and wondered at her name. Strange name for a girl. And isn't it some kind of bird too?

"Then I met Corone when I moved here, and he told me about the Urban Planetbirds. But he never wanted me to…"

"Do me a favor, will you?" Corone turned round. "If you have to go and turn up here, at least keep your endless stories to yourself and just stick to training. All right?"

He flipped his cigarette butt over the wall and jumped after it.

Nobody said anything for a moment.

"He'll calm down," said Jay. "Everything OK?"

Kite was staring at the place where Corone had just been. "Yeah."

It was only now I saw it: her eyes were the least happy I'd ever seen. Well, apart from my ma's eyes maybe, but when you've been walking round on this planet long enough and spent most of that time in the restroom paradise it's pretty difficult to keep your eyes looking happy. Unless you're the Dalai Lama. Boy, did I feel sorry for Kite.

"Corone!" I yelled down over the wall. "We're heading for the stadium, balance practice. You coming?"

"I'm outta here," Corone said back up to me. "It's all too much for me right now."

He didn't look exactly in harmony with the world. And he didn't smell that way either.

Corone smells like a bum, I thought suddenly.

"Would it be better for you if Kite didn't train with us?" I asked quietly. "Be honest. We can break it to her somehow."

"Oh, let her. I'll be OK," said Corone, and sniffed. "It's just right now it's too much." He turned round. "Kittiwake!" he yelled. "Come on, we're going."

Kittiwake came running up.

"Is Mom back?" she asked.

"She's at work."

"Can I go to Jay's pa then? He said he'll give me CDs if I visit him!"

Corone grunted something.

"My father's definitely at home, if that's any help," said Jay.

"All right, then go round to Jay's pa again!" muttered Corone and took Kittiwake's hand. "She's been round there three times now," he said, shaking his head. "Pretty odd couple, huh? Professor Bigshot and the dipshit!"

"I'm the dipshit!" Kittiwake gave a happy laugh.

We all burst out laughing. Even Kite. It did us a whole load of good after all that stress.

"OK, mañana, dude," called Skylark. "Enjoy your organ music, Kittiwake!"

"See ya later." Corone walked off, waving without turning round.

Kittiwake bounced up and down next to him like an outsized rubber ball.

On the way to the stadium, Jay asked, "Hey, is Kite your real name?"

"Yeah, why?"

"Isn't it a bird of prey from the Acciptridae family?"

Woah there. A bird of prey from the Acciptridae family. Jay must have learned that stinky little book by heart.

"A kite's a raptor, like a falcon," said Kite. "Not just a kid's toy."

Yep. The $50,000 sign lit up in my head. Maybe I had what it took to win one of those quiz shows. Then my ma's eyes might get happy in her old age.

"Then you're just perfect for us," I heard Jay saying.

Skylark nodded. "It'd be cool if you joined us. Our token female!"

I took a running jump onto the wall of the bridge across the river. I used a planche to pull myself up onto a little stone tower protruding in the middle, landing precisely on the narrow wall on the other side, with about a fifty-foot drop on my right. Then a saut de fond with a roll-off back onto the sidewalk.

Jay, Skylark, and Kite were walking ahead of me and talking, totally lost in conversation. Cars zoomed past us. I watched Kite from behind them. She looked good when she walked. Like a panther or some other predator when it's not in any rush. She had short hair, reddish brown, and while I'd always thought girls were totally un-feminine when they didn't have long hair, it was different with her. Everything about her looked right. I liked her like crazy.

* * *

Kite kept turning up to training for the next three days. There was something about her that made you really look for your better sides. Or anyway, everyone suddenly started being much nicer. Only Corone and her didn't say a single word to each other. But I saw just how they squinted at each other when the other one wasn't looking. Corone—what an idiot. And I'd always thought I was the only dork around here.

I was always happy when Kite turned up. I talked less when she was there. My heart raced when she stood near me. I thought she was a tiny bit cooler every day. The things she said, like that it smelled of fall, that the seagulls were shining on the river. That kinda thing. And the moment she said anything to me directly, my shirt was soaked with sweat down to my hips. Red alert for Dipper, the king of love!

Yeah, right.

Kittiwake was spending almost all her afternoons with Professor Bigshot. He had a free semester, which means pretty much that you sit in your designer armchair for six months and get boils on your backside because it can't breathe properly. And you read brainy periodicals and grunt a lot, because apparently they only write crap in them. What an impertinence! I heard Professor Bigshot complaining to himself once when Corone and I picked up Kittiwake. What an impertinence! Some people have real bad problems.

Corone was still acting cool and annoyed about Jay's dad, but I could tell he was totally happy to hand Kittiwake over for him to take care of her. I mean, we didn't have to be best buddies with Professor Bigshot—it was enough that Kittiwake was happy there with him. It was really getting too cold outside for her, and like I said, she just got on our nerves when we wanted to concentrate on training. I thought it was pretty tough shit that Corone's ma had to work the late shift all the time. That's no good, I thought back then, if you've got two kids and one of them is Kittiwake. But I didn't say anything. Maybe that was a mistake.

"Guys, I can't make it tomorrow," Jay said that evening. It was dark already and his breath was white under the streetlamp. "I have an essay to work on."

"Yeah, it's that time of year with warm, cozy essays and jolly old grades," said Skylark in a singsong. "Same with me, I'm afraid. So I'm checking out for tomorrow as well, back to the achieving society. Pro parkour, against competition!" He touched fists with Jay.

I could see Corone was gradually realizing who'd be left over.

"Gotta do some spring cleaning tomorrow," he said in a rush. "Our apartment looks like a pigsty."

He shifted his weight from one foot to the other and dragged on his cigarette. The ash glowed orange.

"Can't you do the cleaning on the weekend?" asked Jay.

Corone tossed him a look as black as night.

"Whatever, forget it," said Jay. "So there's just the two of you left." He looked at Kite, then at me. "Maybe you can show Kite a couple of other spots tomorrow, so she knows what's on offer around here. Like private tuition."

Oh boy, I couldn't believe it.

"Sure, I can do that," I said.

My mouth went dry. I had a date.

Corone and Kite squinted at each other for a second.

They'd have been good at poker, that night.

BIRDFEED

I didn't sleep all night long. I lay there, one arm across my eyes, and movies spooled through my head. I was walking through the park with Kite, and at one spot I held a kinda speech, Professor Bigshot–style. Then I showed her the right move for the spot. *How dumb can a movie be?* I thought at some point, tossed and turned onto my side, and thought of something new. Totally in passing, I did a demi-tour over concrete blocks, dropping pearls of wisdom about parkour into the conversation. "You just have to reinterpret your architectural surroundings," I told dream-Kite. I'd heard someone say that on TV, and I was severely impressed. Kite listened admiringly. But then I ran into a street sign and collapsed like a total dork. I tossed and turned onto my other side, thinking, If I keep on like this I'll need crutches to make it to the park tomorrow.

I heard my ma going to the bathroom, and then I heard the kettle boiling in the kitchen. I gave my face another massage and heaved myself out of bed.

"What in God's name are you doing here?" Ma put her hands on her hips, like I was supposed to be on some construction site in Peru and shouldn't just come creeping into the kitchen like that.

"What about you?" I asked her back.

"I've had problems sleeping for twenty years, kid. It's fine for me to sit here at this time of night. Want a coffee?"

She took the kettle and poured water in a cup.

"I'd have problems sleeping too, Ma, if I drank coffee at"—I looked at the kitchen clock above the door to the balcony—"half past three in the morning."

"So what's up with you, honey?"

She sat down opposite me with her steaming coffee cup. I dug away at a notch in the table that some dumb lover of hers had left behind a couple years ago. The guy wanted to show me that trick with the knife and his hand. What a hero.

"Nothing," I said. "Just can't sleep. Got that from you and Pa, I guess."

Ma gave an elephant's slurp at her coffee.

"Baloney! Your father always slept like a dead man, even before he died." She honestly managed to laugh at her strange joke. And because I was so totally, totally tired out of my mind, I joined in.

"C'mon," she said, "tell me what's up, hon. Some girl giving you trouble?"

"That'd be exaggerating."

I got myself the milk out of the icebox.

"Don't drink outta the carton like that!" Ma told me off. "We do have glasses. We're not white trash, you know."

"You sure about that?" I asked.

We giggled again. My ma's really OK. She looked pretty jaded, sitting there with her beloved coffee. I went over to her and pressed her shoulders from behind.

"You're a good boy," she said and patted my hand. "Don't you worry about the girls. You'll find a good 'un. You deserve it."

Oh, Ma.

But the fact was that those couple words from her sent me back to bed in peace, and I slept till my alarm clock rang, like my dead dad before he died.

* * *

On the building site the next day, I worked like a robot. Lugged window frames and sacks of cement up to the fifth floor without even noticing what I was doing.

And then at some point I finally went down to the park. It wasn't bad that I was so tired, 'cause it made me feel more relaxed.

I spotted Kite a long way off. She was wearing something red. I walked up to her, and bang, that was the end of the whole relaxed thing. She watched me walking in her direction with her arms crossed like she was some kind o' prize judge, just about to give me points for how I walked and all that. I tried to walk as casually as I could, but that felt awkward, angular. Behind Kite was the river, and all of a sudden at least a thousand seagulls flew up in the air and were kinda snow-white. And her in red in front. Totally gorgeous.

"Hey," was my totally original greeting.

"Hi," she said.

We touched fists and it felt really strange, as if I was trying to push her away from me.

"So where are we going?" she asked.

"Wherever you wanna go." I really had to give up watching those cheap TV shows. "I mean, I can show you the flower gardens first with a whole load of benches. Good for practicing all sorts of moves."

"Sure."

"We can jog on the way, then we'll warm up," I suggested.

We soon found a rhythm.

"So whaddya do when you're not doing parkour?" she asked.

"I'm working on a construction site right now."

"Aha."

"What about you?"

"Math freshman."

"Wow," I was impressed. "How old are you then?"

"Nineteen." She stopped suddenly. "Wait up a moment, OK?"

There was a little pond on our left. Benches on the right. Kite unzipped her belt bag and took out a handful of something. I couldn't quite see what it was. I stretched my leg against a tree trunk and then took a precision jump onto one of the benches, holding still for a moment. When I looked back over at Kite I thought I was seeing things, I was so tired. But you usually see something different, little white mice or some ghostly pale shadows in the corners of your eyes. What I was seeing was Kite, standing with her arms stretched out and all these birds perched on her hands. They were picking something off her palms and then flying away, and then the next lot of birdies came flying along. I swear I thought I was imagining things again. But actually it was just too gorgeous for my brain. It couldn't have thought up something like that. I stayed in précision, scared this awesome picture might shatter if I jumped down. It was the least ugly picture you've ever seen. Kite looked like an angel. You wanna try that sometime. In sports gear.

"The nuthatches are the freshest." She brushed off her hands. "Wanna try it?"

Now I did jump down off the bench. I don't think I've ever landed so silently.

"OK, why not?" I shrugged.

Kite took a new handful of stuff out of her bag and poured it into my open palm.

"Hold your hand stretched out and upward—like this," she said, showing me what to do.

We waited. Then a bird came up, fluttered up and down crazily by my hand, nervous, and flew away again. Another one did the same.

"Hmm." It was kinda embarrassing standing there like some big friend of the birds, while not one of the damn things would take anything from me.

"They don't know you yet, they don't trust you," Kite explained.

And then she stood right up close to me and put her hand under mine, the one with the birdfeed. I thought I was gonna die right there on the spot. And suddenly my whole body started trembling, all the way to my damn hand. Five seconds later, a pale brown bird with kinda racing stripes on its head came along and set down on my fingertips. Those claws look totally pointy and sharp, but they feel as soft as butter on your hand. And a bird like that weighs something like a quarter of an ounce. More and more birds came over. Kite's hand was real warm; it was like my hand was lying in a nest.

"It's because of you they're not scared," I said.

Kite pulled her hand away from under mine, real softly, as if she didn't want to be cruel and take away the nest too quickly.

"You think so?"

"Sure." I tossed the last few crumbs on the ground. A whole load of pigeons appeared out of nowhere and started pecking their beaks to pieces. "Shall we make a move?"

"I thought we were running?" Kite answers.

Kite laughed and ran off. Me behind her. I couldn't help laughing too. She was running like crazy, and it was only then I realized she was running straight for a tree trunk. What I saw next was faster than anything you've seen before, I swear. She jumped onto the trunk, pushed herself off, landed on a low wall next to it, flipped herself off the other side in a demi-tour, ran a couple yards to the next wall, and jumped over it in a turbo-speed révers. On the grass behind it, she rolled off over her shoulders and stood up neatly.

My jaw dropped. I stood there like someone seeing a traceur in action for the first time. Kite strolled back to me.

"Don't tell Corone, OK?" she said.

"Why not?"

"He doesn't know I've been a traceuse for a couple of years now. He'd be totally frustrated—parkour's his big thing."

I was still stunned like crazy by what I'd just seen.

"D'you get it?" she asked.

"No," I said. "You're not stopping him from training, are you?"

"Of course not. But he already feels inferior all the time. And if I suddenly come along and say, parkour, hey sure, I do that too, I'll be straight out the door for him."

I'd thought they were finished with each other anyway. Funny, huh?

"If you say so," I said doubtfully. "But it's a shame, you're real talented. You have to keep on training, jeez!"

"It's OK," she said. "And thanks for the compliment."

She smiled at me all of a sudden, and I think that was the first time we ever looked each other in the eyes. Properly, I mean. I couldn't take it—I looked away like greased lightning.

We did another hour's training. I totally felt like showing her stuff now, and she did a couple moves for me too and gave me a couple tips.

"The best thing about parkour is that now I don't see obstacles in my way anymore, all I see is possibilities. And it's kinda extended to my whole life. Even math. I just keep thinking, I'm gonna solve this problem, no matter how."

She was sitting next to me on a bench, drinking out of my water bottle.

"I have another hobby, you know," she said, handing me the bottle.

As I drank, I thought that her mouth was kinda on mine now, via a slight detour.

"What is it?"

"Shall I show you? Are you really interested?"

"Sure."

"How about tomorrow? After training? At my place?"

Oh boy, what a day!

Maybe Ma'd been right the night before.

About not worrying about girls.

Or so I thought.

BREAKING THROUGH

The next day we got unlucky: ticket inspectors on the way to the old trade fair. Corone didn't have a ticket. So he started rummaging wildly through all the pockets in his jacket and pants in front of the two guys.

"That's funny," he said. "I had it a minute ago."

"Then we'll have to see some ID," croaked the short fat one of the two inspectors standing in front of Corone's seat, like Laurel and Hardy or something.

"But I gotta get off next stop, I'm in a hurry." Corone looked totally panicked all of a sudden; I mean, they were only ticket inspectors. He usually kept his cool with stuff like that.

We all acted like we didn't know him. We'd been through the routine a thousand times before 'cause he never bought a ticket. I noticed Kittiwake taking a breath to say something to Corone, and I put a quick hand over her mouth, not too conspicuously. Then I stared at her like one of those hypnotist guys, and slowly let go again.

"We're not letting you off until we've seen some ID," said Laurel.

The train stopped with a screech. The doors hissed open. Corone ducked under Laurel's arm, dodged past Hardy, and jumped up on a strap hanging from the ceiling. From there, he swung himself out of the doors: saut de fond and a roll across the street. The doors slurped shut right in front of Laurel and Hardy's noses.

"Would you believe it?" said Laurel.

"They get fresher every day," said Hardy. "And they don't take a shower either. That kid smelled like my grandpa."

Behind their backs, we signaled to Corone that he should catch up with us later.

Kite watched him for longer than the rest of us; I saw her.

"But I've got a ticket," Kittiwake whispered.

"That's good, Princess," said Jay.

Kittiwake sat down on Jay's lap and we all showed our tickets.

Kite looked at me. My heart beat faster, and I made an attempt to smile as best I could. I was looking forward like crazy to visiting her later.

"Have you got thinner?" Jay asked suddenly, looking more closely at Kittiwake.

"Don't know," she answered.

"Don't you guys think she looks much thinner?" Jay stroked Kittiwake's hair.

"Yeah," nodded Skylark.

He was right. Kittiwake was thinner. And she was pale too. But at least she seemed clean, which was more than you could say about her brother.

"Are you eating properly?" Jay asked her.

Kittiwake gave a silent nod.

"I heard you and my dad are clearing out our attic," Jay tried again.

Kittiwake nodded again but didn't say a word.

Then we had to get off the train.

The old trade fair was as empty as if it had died. As if someone had totally evacuated all the people. The flags outside the supermarket jangled and squeaked. Long rows of shopping carts were parked under glass roofs. The wind was icy, and dark clouds hung in the sky. Fat, ominous clouds.

Corone came jogging round the corner. At our favorite spot he, Jay, and Skylark jumped onto an arcade pillar one after another, trying to do a tic-tac over to a railing and add a franchissement through it onto the end. It had to be a pretty precise move. While they were at it, I "showed" Kite how to balance along the rail. One foot in front of the other, spreading her arms. If you lose your balance, bend your knees as best you can and then saut de fond, jump to the ground with a bounce.

I held her hand. She gave a slightly over-the-top waver and leaned on my hand, and I held hers tight, tighter than she'd have needed it for équilibre. She laughed and we looked at each other, and I was happy because she was so cute and because I was the only one who knew she was faking it all. Then I showed her how to balance along the rail on all fours. She copied me in a totally awesome way, and sadly I didn't need to hold on to any little bit of her. I really noticed how she sometimes forgot to play the rookie, because she was just totally perfect then. Boy, was she an awesome traceuse! I couldn't get it into my head why she had to hide it from Corone. Once she even fell off the rail deliberately and yelled out a bit and all that. Corone looked over at us, but the two of them hadn't said a single word to each other since we'd met up. I was glad about that. And apart from that I was totally wired.

"I'm gonna go practice franchissement now, OK?" I said after a while, 'cause I thought the guys might have noticed me just messing about here with Kite and neglecting my training.

"No problem, Dipper."

I felt like a million dollars every time she said my name.

It's a real cool feeling when you think you're never gonna get a jump or a combination down right, or not till next summer or something, and then you stand there and after the twentieth move you flick some kind of switch in your head. You run, push off, and swing in a perfect motion between the bars of a railing, as if you were Cyril Raffaelli in *Banlieue 13* for a second of your life. Makes for major satisfaction.

We were completely concentrated that evening, totally at one with what we were doing. It was almost like magic. You get days like that when something suddenly falls into place, something that hadn't made the slightest bit of progress for ages. As if you'd just been a caterpillar in a cocoon for the longest time, and all of a sudden you break out of your shell. And fly. And then there was Kite's smile. I was happy, I guess.

"Where's my sister, by the way?" Corone asked abruptly. He was right. I hadn't seen her for a while either.

"Kittiwake!" he yelled.

We all ran away from the spot and out into this weird dusky, almost vanished light. There was an earthy smell of rotting leaves, as if something was dying. Crows were stalking around. But no sign of Kittiwake.

We yelled and looked, looked and yelled. No answer. Nada. Only the flagpoles jangling and the icy wind blowing.

We spread right out across the area. It was like the ground had opened up and swallowed Kittiwake.

Fifteen minutes later, Kite found her behind a trashcan. Kittiwake had grabbed an old pack of chips outta there and was crunching them down. I swear I thought I was seeing things. The whole thing made me kinda sad, all of a sudden. The way she was squatting down there. With a lousy pack of chips.

"Hey, we've been looking for you everywhere!" Corone grabbed her by the arm. "Put that shit down right now, man!"

"I'm not a man!" Kittiwake dropped her chips and started to cry. "I wanna go home! I'm cold!"

"OK, OK, chillax, kid, we're going already," said Corone.

"We could all come back with you and watch videos on the net," Sky suggested. "I haven't seen what the cracks are at for a while now."

Jay nodded. "I'm in," he said. "I heard there's some new stuff from a couple of Spanish girls, traceuses from Madrid, I think. Supposed to be genius material."

"Sorry, guys, not with me today," Corone interrupted. "You can see what's up with my sister, I have to take care of her. Maybe next time."

"I could put Kittiwake to bed, then you'd have less work to do," said Jay. "What do you say, Princess?" he asked Kittiwake. "Want me to?"

I was already amazed that Corone and Jay hadn't had one bust-up that day. But you shouldn't count your chickens before they're hatched, says my ma, because there's always someone who pees on the seat at the end of the day, just when you've rinsed out your cleaning cloth to go home.

"I just said no," barked Corone.

"Is Jay gonna put me to bed?" Kittiwake was hopping up and down next to Jay, suddenly as happy as ever.

"I said no," Corone said again.

He took his sister's hand, turned on his heel, and left without one more damn word.

ORIGAMI

Kite and I headed for an elevator in the semi-darkness. A button lit up red when she pressed it, and there was an instant low sound of creaking and buzzing.

"Are your parents home?" I asked her.

The whole first-contact-to-parents thing is always so dumb.

"I live on my own," she said. "My parents are back in Wales, where I'm from. I'm here to study."

"How come you speak such good German?"

I realized I was breaking out in a sweat, 'cause, oh boy, an apartment with no Mas and Pas and then a girl like this. The elevator showed up with a dull plop and the doors slid apart. If Kite hadn't been there I'd have played at Darth Vader; I always do that in elevators. But I got my act together.

"My mother's German," she said. The doors closed behind us. "I learned both languages, or actually three: German, Welsh, and English."

"Cool," I said.

The elevator buzzed us up to the fifth floor.

When we got out and walked along a dark corridor past rows and rows of doors with no names on them, I didn't feel one bit like Darth Vader. More like Milhouse Van Houten. Kite stopped at the very last door, unlocked it, and nudged me in. Flicked on the light.

"It's just a tiny apartment, but it's all in one room," she said.

"Even the toilet?" I asked, genuinely horrified for a moment.

"No, come on!" Kite laughed and flicked on another light behind a door. "The toilet's in a separate room, don't worry."

Listen up, everyone! Dipper's showing off his skills again. What to say when you meet your dream girl. The tongue in my mouth was clearly not put there for talking with.

"I'll make us a hot drink, OK?" she said.

"OK."

I followed her, and found myself in a huge room. Opposite me a row of windows as long as the wall, behind them a balcony. I wouldn't want to carry those windows up here, I thought; the frames were enormous. On the right was a folded-out couch, next to it a desk with a computer on it and loads of stuff, papers and pens and all that. Apart from that, I only saw one thing in the whole damn room: paper shapes. They were dangling from the ceiling, lying on the floor, and covering the couch. Everywhere. I took a couple steps, then I thought I'd better take my shoes off, or I'd squash something with my parkour sneakers.

"Oh, that's nice of you," I heard Kite. "D'you drink coffee?"

"Only at three in the morning with my ma," I said.

Kite laughed. "Shall I make us hot chocolate?"

"Hot chocolate would be awesome," I said.

She clattered around and I walked across the room. A gray angel made of tiny paper folds floated in front of my face. I gave it a tap and it started to swing. Next to it dangled some kind of small tree trunk with a green insect perched on it, with a zillion tiny legs and its wings pressed back. What the hell was going on here?

"It's origami," said Kite, just as I was inspecting a little man on the back of a dragon, looking like they'd come riding straight out of some fantasy film. "The art of paper folding."

She came up to me and handed me a steaming cup.

"Thanks."

I glugged at it right away and burnt my tongue. Damn! There was something wrong with that part of my anatomy today. I closed my eyes for a moment, waiting for the pain to die down.

"You OK?" asked Kite.

"Yeah, everything's fine."

"I'm kinda obsessed with it," explained Kite, picking up a paper figure and turning it round in front of our faces. "This butterfly here is folded out of one square of paper, without making a single cut."

She put it down on my free hand.

"You mean everything, the wings, the feelers, the head, is made out of one sheet of paper?"

"That's right."

She sat down on the big dark red rug on the wooden floor, and I sat down with her. I was still balancing the butterfly on my hand. I took a sip of hot chocolate, now that my tongue was scalded anyway, but my malfunctioning anatomy still noticed it tasted like manna from heaven. Nothing like all the other hot chocolates in all my miserable little Dipper life.

"What's in it?" I asked, raising my cup.

43

"Pepper," said Kite.

Then she explained, "You know, one of the great origami masters, Robert Lang, is a physicist. He developed about five hundred of these amazing paper figures. It has a lot to do with geometry. The rule is: only one sheet of paper and no cuts or tears."

She looked at me as if I might have a gift for her, and she expected me to whip it out and hand it to her at any moment. But I didn't have one.

"Does that remind you of anything? Or is it just me with my theory?"

She kept on looking at me in that crazy way.

Oh boy, I felt like I was on a quiz show again. This must have been about, let's say, the $80,000 question.

"So," I gave it a try, "these origami guys make all this out of one sheet of paper, with no tools?"

"Yes."

"So they have a goal and they go straight there without getting distracted? A path with no diversions?"

"Yes!"

"Paper parkour," I said.

Kite looked at me. She was grinning a thousand times more than Kittiwake at an organ session or my ma when she unwrapped her heated pillow. I turned around, thinking it must be something behind my back making her so happy. But there was only a wall behind me.

"That's just what I think too!" she said. "And think about it: two Japanese guys derived seven basic axioms that all folding processes can be reduced to, that bring the points and lines together on one level. And Robert Lang proved there isn't a single conceivable fold that can't be described by the seven fundamental axioms."

Boy, oh boy. My respect for this girl had just increased to the monumental proportions of the monster wall. That was the least fluffed spontaneous presentation I'd ever heard. And it wasn't just blah, all that stuff Kite had just said. I mean, I didn't quite get what it all meant, but something inside me swung open like a saloon door and a breath of fresh air blew over me.

"Did you make them all yourself?" I asked her.

"Yeah, they're all mine."

She picked up the butterfly from my hand, and we touched for a moment. We looked at each other, right in the eyes. Her gaze shot straight to my stomach. Kite went over to her desk and put the paper figure down carefully.

"Origami helps train your concentration. And that's what we traceurs and traceuses do too."

The way she was leaning against the desk like that, one leg crossed over the other and one arm under her elbow, I must have been staring at her by accident.

"What are you looking at?" she asked.

"Me? Nothing," I shot out. "I was just thinking about your two Japanese guys and all that, with their theory."

Was I really Milhouse and she was Lisa Simpson?

"The Huzita-Hatori Axioms, right," she said, more to herself than to me, which didn't bother me.

She put her cup down on the desk.

"You know, it's all advanced mathematics, I don't understand it either. I just wanted to show you, because I always thought there was some kind of parallel."

Kite lay down on the rug and folded her arms behind her head. It was a bit like Jay did. Probably all real clever people lie down on some damn rug at least once a day, no matter where they come across one.

I don't know, somehow I felt like lying down as well. With me, it was more like after all the lugging of windows and cement sacks and the peppery hot chocolate—that sort of wanting to lie down. So I lay on the floor a little way away from Kite. Between us was a paper crab.

"Hey, have you ever been to Corone's place?" she asked.

"No, not yet. Why?"

Kite sighed.

"I just think it's strange. We were together for three months and he wouldn't let me visit once. There was always something up: one time it was too messy, then Kittiwake was supposedly sick, then his mother had some guy round, then this, then that. It totally upset me, as if he wanted to hide something from me. Not show me how he really is. D'you get it?"

"I can imagine it, yeah."

Now that Kite mentioned it, I realized that Corone had really never taken us back home with him. To be honest, I didn't even know exactly where he lived.

She turned on her side and looked at me. With her gorgeous, gorgeous eyes.

"I think that might even be why he split up with me. He doesn't want to let anyone see the real him. I'm worried about him. Maybe you and me could go round there together sometime soon. Would you come with me?"

I turned on my side. "We'll see if he lets us in." I grinned. "No, sure, let's do it. I'll help you. My pleasure, really."

Kite picked up the crab from the rug between us and put it down behind her. Then she sat up right close to me with her legs crossed, took my head in her hands, and kissed my hair.

"Thanks, Dipper, you're a real sweet guy," she said. "You know, Corone's still important to me, as a friend. He's been my only little island since I arrived in Germany, all on my own without my family and all that."

"Mhm," I said and nodded, even though I didn't think what she was telling me was all that great. I had a feeling on the top of my head from her kiss as if a butterfly had settled there, if not an angel. Maybe both.

Suddenly Kite grinned.

"Can you teach me tic-tac at our next training session?" she asked.

"What?"

"Can you teach me tic-tac?"

She suddenly leapt to her feet and rolled her torso upward, one vertebra at a time. She looked as smooth as a cat.

I got up too. "But you can do tic-tac better than me."

She tipped her head and gave me a big, knowing wink. Two seconds later, I got the hint. "Oh sure, you still wanna keep your traceuse skills under wraps, right?"

She nodded, smiled, and stood there without talking.

"I'll be going then," I said after a while.

"Yeah."

She walked me to the door.

I really didn't want to go.

I had my hand on the door handle when she hugged me from behind. Totally unexpectedly.

I turned around to her.

Her face was floating right up close below mine.

And then I kissed her.

We must have stood there at the door like that for at least ten minutes. If Kite hadn't led me by the hand back toward her room, I'd probably still be standing there right now.

One second later, we were lying on the folded-out couch.

I don't know for sure, but I think the world kinda disappeared all of a sudden. Like someone had zipped it off all round us. All I saw was Kite, all I tasted was her face, and all I smelled was her hair. She had her hands in my hair and her mouth on my mouth, on my eyes, my ears. She whispered stuff. I whispered her name. She stroked around my lips with her fingers.

Being so close to her. Touching her like this.

It made me go extra-terrestrial.

This is so totally outta this world, I thought.

At some point she started taking her clothes off.

"What's with you?" she whispered, sitting naked in front of me. Just beautiful.

I stared at her.

No world anymore.

"Hey you," she said quietly, and pulled my sweatshirt over my head.

How can I describe what came next?

One thing: my heart must have been beating like some pretty awesome hammer percussion.

Or was it not my heart?

NIAGARA FALLS

"Honey, I'm getting worried about you."

Ma was standing there, the kettle in her hand still whooshing away like Niagara Falls (those cheap electric kettles are mighty loud), when I came in the kitchen the next night.

"I'll have a coffee too," I said, rubbing my eyes.

It was three thirty in the middle of the night, just like last time we'd met up in the kitchen. Seemed like we could start up a club.

"Hey, c'mon, out with it." Ma put a hot cup of coffee down in front of me. "What's up?"

Some huge plane flew over our house, sounding like when you get too close to a Bunsen burner. They'd rerouted the flight path right over our heads that spring. Thanks a bundle.

I hadn't even answered when Ma leaned back in her quilted robe that she'd had for about a hundred and fifty years, and said: "You're in love, I can tell."

It was three thirty in the morning and I looked like I was in love. You wanna try that sometime.

"Oh, I don't know…" I tried to twist out of it, like a verbal demi-tour.

"But I know." Ma slurped at her coffee. "And does the girl like you back?"

I made the world's most doubtful face and shrugged. Then I submerged as much of myself as possible in my coffee cup.

"So you don't know that," she said with a nod.

I emerged from my cup, and suddenly, no idea why, I started telling my ma everything. About Corone. About Kite. And about the two of us hanging out together. Then I told her about origami and the two Japanese guys and everything. Well, I left out the last part. I'm not so good at describing that extra-terrestrial stuff. Ma listened to me like nothing on Earth. Sometimes she took a slurp of her coffee, then she raised her eyebrows, then she smiled, then she nodded or shook her head. I talked and talked, chatted her ear right off, and somehow I just couldn't stop. But it didn't bother her none at all. She listened like I was talking in Robert De Niro's voice or something. When I got to the end I looked at my coffee, and I could tell it had cooled down to about 35 degrees. Ma got up, shuffled over to the kettle, and switched it back on.

"Honey," she said over the sound of Niagara Falls, "you're gonna have to fight for that girl."

She dumped a couple spoons of coffee granules in a new cup and poured water on them. I gotta get her a coffee maker.

"You think?" I asked.

"She likes you, that's for sure," said Ma. "You're halfway there. But she's not over your friend yet, I guess. She wants to help him."

"So how am I supposed to fight for her?"

"Just show her what you can do, hon. You've got plenty to show for yourself."

???

By the time we'd finished our coffee it was five o'clock.

I hit the sack for another hour. I think I slept as deep as my dead dad, after he died.

* * *

I'm standing on a roof, nothing below me, no hold, no ground. I'm standing on the edge and I can see the next roof. Below me, an ambulance wails past, something jangles and clatters. A plane comes closer and closer, then flies crazy low across the roof I'm standing on, looking out over the rows of buildings. I'm scared. Not just any old fear, the kind you can breathe away. Everything inside me is fear, one big huge knot, my whole body totally paralyzed. That's how I'm standing there. Alone.

I know I have to get across, to the other damn distant side. I know it, I have no choice but to take the leap, but I can't. I can't damn well move a single inch of my body. Totally frozen. Wind whips at my hair, a couple raindrops spit in my face like they're making fun of me. I can't jump. I'm falling. I'm falling.

I hear someone crying. The wind hurls scraps of the sound at me, a crying I've heard before.

Kittiwake, I think. Kiddo?

Then I see her, over on the other roof. She's squatting down behind a chimney, and something's flying around above her head and thrusting down at her, black and screaming.

"Kittiwake!"

I shout like crazy. I see the crow getting caught up in Kittiwake's hair and hacking at her face, hacking mercilessly at the little girl crouching there in a ball, holding her hands in front of her face now and crying.

I'm standing there. I'm standing at the edge, nothing below me, no ground, no hold. Something inside me flinches, but I can't do it. I scream…

"Dipper!"

My T-shirt soaked in sweat. The cover hot and sticky on top of me. My booming heart.

"Honey, you gotta get up, you've overslept."

Ma pulled the blind up with a whiz, and I blinked.

I'm here. Mercy, I'm here.

"You were tossing and turning and moaning," said Ma, looking at me and sighing. "OK now?"

"Yeah." I levered myself out of bed.

What kind of a crappy dream was that? A hundred percent horror. Why did I dream about Kittiwake? I'd rather have dreamed of Kite.

"Gotta run, got a long day today," said Ma, and I heard her putting on her jacket outside my room. "Look out for yourself when you're hopping about on your walls out there, OK?"

"Sure, Ma, I'll look after myself."

DISCIPLINE

After work I went straight into town and bought origami paper for Kite. The saleswoman explained a thousand things, but I wasn't even listening. I just looked at the brightly colored paper, and who knows how many butterflies, angels, and dragons started fluttering around inside my head.

When I got to the park I heard Corone saying, "No, boot camps are awesome!"

He jumped from a standing position into précision and counted his steps back to the jump-off mark. "Seven feet, man! I've got a whole foot better these last few weeks."

That was saying something, what with the size of his huge feet. I could make just about six foot-lengths, but only on a good day. Usually more like five and a half.

"Man, comrade," Skylark said, "what kind of fascist trip are you on now?" He jumped, landed on the balls of his feet, and tried to hold his position, but then tipped to one side.

"Just let up with your comrade crap, OK?" Corone growled at him. "If you went to one of those camps for a while you wouldn't be such a pathetic spaz as you are now!"

"Hey, I can't believe the crap you're talking, Corone," said Skylark. "You think it's awesome when a bunch of military assholes demoralize kids so badly they end up running round like robots? Your brawn may be OK, but you're lacking in the brains department."

He balanced on the sidings around a flowerbed, jumped, and landed precisely on the opposite edge.

"Let's train at another spot today, OK?" Corone suggested. "I've had enough of doing the same crap here all the time."

"So where you wanna go?" I asked.

"I'll just go water the flowers, then I'll show you the place. Wall, Ping-Pong table for double chat, it's all there."

He disappeared behind a couple bushes.

I looked around. Kite wasn't there yet. It was gonna be weird seeing her again, after yesterday and everything. I was pretty nervous.

"Comrade Corone's starting to worry me with his funny comments," said Skylark.

Sky was wearing a black sweatshirt with a white print on it, the name of a band: The Fat Policeman. On the back it said: "Hated, damnated, relegated." There was a pin on his beanie: "No Person Is Illegal." Skylark was a walking billboard that day.

Then Kite came jogging round the corner.

"Sorry, my seminar overran," she said.

"A little more discipline wouldn't do any harm, young lady." Corone came out of the bush, fumbling at the bib of his overalls.

Kite said hi to Sky and Jay—and smiled at me. Kinda friendly or something. And then? She stopped yards away from me. Between me and Corone. She didn't take one step in my direction. My heart hammered away. I smiled back, feeling like Bozo the Clown a second later. What was this all about? After yesterday and everything? What was going on here? I thought she'd come over to me any moment. But instead, she started chatting with Skylark. Laughing. First I felt like a bug on its back. I floundered around, inside, but that didn't help one bit. Then I felt something soft or liquid going hard as rock inside of me. This lump between my ribs. Like tar. I didn't know if I should go over to her or not. So I didn't. The sun was low in the sky. I looked into it, and then all I could see was dark spots. Once I could see properly again, I noticed there were hardly any leaves left on the trees. Everything was bare; black octopus arms against a blue sky.

"C'mon, it's a fifteen-minute run!" Corone gestured at us to follow him.

We made a move.

I didn't know anymore how I felt. I was empty or something. So empty that anything could happen. Anything.

The river that day looked the way I imagine the sea in summer. Hundreds of seagulls perched on it, swaying to and fro. We all shuffled our sneakers through the piles of leaves. I took extra-hard kicks, bang, bang, over and over, as if I was shooting balls into oblivion with all my might. When Kite suddenly showed up next to me, our long shadows touched on the sidewalk.

She glanced over at Corone, then at me.

"Here," she whispered, passing me something.

It was a folded sheet of paper, a tiny ship. I shoved it in the pocket of my fleece jacket, realizing I was suddenly nervous as hell. And I wasn't even doing anything bad! Kite was acting like we were in jail and had five minutes in the yard to exchange surreptitious messages. You wanna try that sometime—even though we were actually totally free and everything. OK, I thought, at least she's given you something. I wanted to take her hand, but she flinched and went over to Jay. The day before, we'd been closer than anyone can be. And now all I got was a piece of paper?

We were soon jogging down streets where the residents aren't quite so rich and famous, more like regulars in the welfare line. And suddenly we saw Jay clambering up a facade like a monkey. The wall had the perfect moldings on it, pretty much begging to be climbed up. When Jay reached the third floor, a window opened and a guy put his head out.

"What the hell are you doing there?" he yelled, and I could see even from the ground that he only had three or four teeth left growing in his mouth garden. Woah there. "Go on, scram, goddamn!"

Jay scrambled down at turbo-speed.

"Guess he was an out-of-work poet," was his dry comment.

We laughed. When I looked at Kite and her sparkling eyes and her mouth and when she looked at me, for a moment it was like there was a link between us. A link that couldn't be cut. Made of fine metal. Silver. My heart drummed beneath the lump like a prisoner beating at his cell door.

"C'mon, let's get going again, guys!" complained Corone.

He was laying down some heavy stress, I thought.

"What, you don't have five minutes for a little joke?" asked Skylark. "We're the urban scrammers, man!" He laughed so hard he folded in two and had to rest his hands on his knees.

"Don't wet your pants!" Corone said. Not moving a muscle in his face, he carried on jogging, right across the street, Kite in tow. And us behind them. "You know what'd be

awesome? If we had T-shirts printed with a logo for the
Urbans. And if we trained harder. Man, there are traceurs out
there who train so hard they barf! And us? Remedial level."

Nobody said anything. We jogged on at normal speed,
between two blocks of houses, along a footpath, on our left
and right grass littered with cans and empty cigarette packs.
Kite stumbled, and Corone grasped her under the arms in
passing, as if she was his property. Keep your hands off her,
I thought.

"So what should be on these shirts, in your humble opin-
ion?" Skylark asked at last. "Urban fuckin' Disciplines, or
what?"

"Well, certainly not a crock of crap like on yours!"

"Don't talk shit, Corone! You need to do some ethi-
cal and moral sobering up—and not in one of your boot
camps!" said Skylark.

The footpath ended on a street that was strangely
quiet—no traffic, I mean. I always notice that kinda thing
real fast.

Less than three seconds later we spotted two dark green
vans, and next to them a bunch of cops togged out in full
body armor. They were all looking in one direction, down
the street. To be precise, they were looking in our direction.
They were all clutching big black helmets to their stomachs,
as if they thought someone wanted to take them away from
them.

We crossed the street, and luckily we were out of their
sights half a minute later.

"What're they waiting for?" Skylark jumped over a rail.

"Who knows?" said Jay. "Maybe it's some kind of emergency drill?" He followed in révers.

"What kind of emergency?" I asked him, balancing along the rail on all fours and then jumping down to the street. I'd already spotted the second set of switched-off traffic lights.

"Who cares, it's nothing to do with us." Kite weaved her body between the rails.

"There's the spot over there," Corone called out.

We jogged across the street.

I swear not a single car passed us.

That silence made me suspicious.

RUN

The spot was perfect. It had pretty much everything to warm a traceur's heart: two benches, a concrete Ping-Pong table, a wall about six feet high. Behind the wall came a stretch of scrubby grass.

"Hey great, at least nobody can stare at us here," I said.

We piled up our bags. Skylark levered himself over the wall and disappeared out of sight, Corone sat himself down on top of it with his legs dangling. I crouched down behind the Ping-Pong table and took the paper ship out of my pocket. I just had to know what Kite had written me. I didn't have the patience to wait till that evening. Like a prize idiot, I started unfolding the thing, and unfolding and unfolding. I gave a quiet curse, thinking, An e-mail's sure easier to open.

"Get down, right now!"

It certainly wasn't any of our voices. Before I'd even read a single word I crumpled up the paper, stuffed it in my jacket and stood up behind the table.

In front of me were about fifteen cops.

"And you get back here off the grass, move it!"

Skylark climbed over the wall with a skilled move and leapt down in front of the policemen's noses. Suddenly the slogan on his sweatshirt seemed pretty grotesque. Corone slid down the wall in slow motion.

My stomach lurched, no kidding. All around us suddenly these huge great guys, their armored uniforms so bulky they looked like they were twice as broad as they were tall. One uniform held up a video camera and trained it right on all of us. None of us said a word. Kite looked over at me, her eyes as fearful as you can get.

"IDs!" barked the tallest uniform.

I saw the riot stick and the weapon dangling off him. The helmet under his arm. OK, I thought. Chillax, Dipper. I scrabbled around for my ID, Jay and Kite rifling through their pockets. Out of the corner of my eye, I noticed the look on Corone's face. Total panic. A whole lot worse than with the ticket inspectors the day before. What was up with him? Something wasn't right.

"You're suspected of trespassing, just for your information!" the cop croaked.

Trespassing?

The guy sounded so much like a robot that it gave me goose bumps. I'd have paid a whole lotta money to find out how to switch him off. No one had asked us yet what we were actually doing there. Why the hell were they treating us like serious criminals?

"I don't have my ID card on me," I heard Corone say.

"Then show us some other form of ID."

I swear I couldn't tell which of the uniforms said what, they all looked and sounded exactly the same.

"What's going on here, officers?" I asked.

I really wanted to know, and at the same time I wanted to distract them from Corone, who was hunting frantically through his backpack.

"You know exactly what's going on!" droned one of the cops.

I swear I thought I was in some kind of movie, and then I thought, no, this isn't a movie, these are the outtakes, the bits left over from the real story that end up on the cutting-room floor.

"You come with me!" One of the uniforms pointed at Skylark.

"Hey, peace, man, we're just doing parkour. Is that illegal now?"

The cop grabbed Sky below the elbow and shoved him toward the street.

"Don't touch me!" hissed Sky.

The uniform with the video camera was walking alongside them. I saw them push Sky inside a police van.

Corone still hadn't produced any "other form of ID." But he had gone red in the face and broken out in a sweat on his top lip, glittering in the light of a streetlamp. I had to distract the uniforms from Corone.

I reached for my belt bag, took out my cell phone and held it to my ear.

"Yes?" I said and took an artificial pause. "No, we're in Biedermannstrasse."

"Hang up—right now!"

The cop grabbed me by the ear, no kidding, trying to tear the phone out of my hand. I twisted out of his grasp and said into the phone again: "Biedermannstrasse. You guys come by, OK?"

"You are in a police check!" yelled the cop, and tried again to grab the phone out of my hand.

"I can talk on my phone as long as I like!" I yelled back. "You think I'm setting off a bomb here by cell phone, or what?"

"Could well be."

The guy seemed real nervous now, kept looking over at his colleagues standing lined up in front of us. He planted himself right next to me and stared me in the face.

"Have I got shit on my face?" I asked.

"Look in the mirror," he answered.

I walked a couple yards away and took my phone out of my bag again.

"Yeah, Dipper here," I said into it.

I saw the cop pulling on his second leather glove.

"I'm not gonna tell you again."

He walked toward me, deliberately slowly. I took advantage of the moment to look over at Corone. I looked him more firmly in the eye than ever before. Something flickered in his face.

Then I ran for it.

I jumped over two benches and across the metal rail dividing the spot from the street.

"Stay where you are! Stay where you are!"

I ran.

"Diiipppeeer!"

That was Kite's voice. I turned around mid-run.

I saw one of the cops aiming something at me with outstretched arms. Behind him, the whole bunch of uniforms broke into a run. And in a fraction of a second, I noticed Corone too, jumping over a wall somewhere far back and disappearing. Like an animal, I ducked down low and moved faster, crazy fast, faster than I'd ever run before.

Something whizzed through the air. I pulled my head in. Two projectiles fell on the sidewalk next to me. Tasers. Oh man, just how serious was this crap? At that moment, sirens wailed out. A police car turned onto the street directly in front of me, braking sharply. Two cops leapt out. One pointed another weapon at me.

"Stay where you are!"

The cops weren't even ten yards away from me, and that was nothing for one of those damn Tasers, I knew it. I looked to the left and suddenly spotted a wire fence. I took a run-up, jumped as high as I could, climbed, threw my body over the fence, my fingers grabbing at the wire, I dropped down and rolled off, ran again.

I heard them stopping suddenly behind me; one of them kicked the fence and cursed. Stupidly enough, I realized I'd landed in a backyard, facades on the left and right, a wall in front of me. The wall was too high for passe muraille, but there was a lightning conductor in one corner. I climbed up it at turbo-speed, hearing the cops jabbering into their walkie-talkies as if through a fog. There was a van parked on the other side of the wall. I jumped. Landed in a crouch on the roof of the van. A dog started barking and a window was wrenched open somewhere.

"Hey! What's going on?!" shouted a man's voice.

I didn't look up, jumping down from the van. I was in yet another damn backyard. I tore open a door, took a giant leap over a child sitting on a toy car in the corridor, tore open the front door, and was back on the street.

I kept running until I came to a wheezing stop at a play area, what felt like hours later. I bent over and rested my hands on my thighs. I breathed and breathed. White clouds in the dark before my face.

I calmed down after a couple minutes.

I took a careful look round. But no one was there. Not one cop, not one person.

I walked slowly over to a swing, sat down, and hooked my elbows round the chains. It was comforting swinging to and fro. I felt like I was in my aunt's garden, a thousand years ago. My father was pushing me on the swing and I was happy.

By the time I could breathe normally again, there was only one thought in my mind: Kite had warned me when I was in danger. She'd called my name.

I pulled my rescued ID card out of my jacket, then the crumpled paper ship. By the light of the streetlamp, I read Kite's handwriting.

Shadow Blues (by Laura Veirs)
There's a shadow beneath the sea
There's a shadow between you and me
I've learned that love is scared of light
Thousand seeds from a flower
Blowing through the night
Your blackened kiss on my cheek
Your blackened kiss runs river deep
A stranded fish, dear, I'm on sand
Blue water from a pool
Up to the clouds I'll land
Though I am dark 'bout the whys of wanting
Though I am dark, I'm still a child
Gonna dig a coal mine, climb down deep inside
Where my shadow's got one place to go
One place to hide …

KAFKA

"It's unbelievable!" Skylark threw down the newspaper between us on the mattresses. "I don't know whether to laugh or barf!"

We were hanging in the old trade fair hall, to debrief after everything that had happened. The article had finally shed some light on why we'd got caught up in that dumb police check: a neo-Nazi party had opened an office, right in the building we'd wanted to train behind, and right at the moment we'd showed up there.

"That's what I'd call bad timing," Jay said.

"Their timing or ours?" I asked.

"Jeez, guys, I felt like something outta Kafka's *Trial*!" Skylark said, excitedly. "I'm sitting there in that damn van and telling them about parkour, and they keep on saying: 'You know perfectly well why you're here.' And I didn't know shit. It was a hundred percent horror!" He jumped up from the mattress and paced to and fro. "It's a total nightmare. You find yourself somewhere, you have no idea what's going on, and suddenly you're supposed to be some kinda left-wing terrorist!" Then he launched himself onto the mattress again and rubbed his face with both hands.

"I told you guys we should make ourselves parkour shirts. Then they'd at least have seen who we were," said

Corone. "No wonder they thought we were suspicious, what with your dumb sweatshirt slogans."

"Hey, I can wear whatever dumb sweatshirts I like. It doesn't give them the right to frame me for anything, OK?" answered Skylark.

"So did you guys run away as well?" I asked.

"We couldn't, they still had our ID cards," said Jay.

"Yeah, and then they wanted us to tell them you guys' names and addresses," Kite chipped in. She looked totally wiped out. Pale was not the word. She was white as a sheet. I'd have liked to hug her, but she'd sat down much too far away from me again. "But we just said we didn't know you, you were new in the group and all that."

"And they actually believed you?" asked an irritated Corone.

Jay shrugged. "What else could they do? They just warned us and ordered us to move on. And then they let us go." He looked at me. "You didn't necessarily have to launch an uprising like that, Dipper. It just made the situation even more tense. The cops weren't exactly friendlier to us after your action-movie escape. What was that all about?"

I tried to meet Corone's eyes, and before I'd thought of anything cool to say, he piped up, "Man, Jay! It was totally awesome, Dipper's whole number. That was parkour!"

"Bullshit," said Sky.

Kite didn't say anything. But she kept looking over at me.

"And Tasers, guys," said Skylark, "that's totally off the scale."

"Why? They're not dangerous," said Corone. "Only the special police squads use them." He grinned.

He was kinda starting to annoy me. I mean, I'd really rescued him out of deep shit, using every muscle in my little Dipper body, and he was sitting there grinning and defending the Tasers that had damn near pumped my ass full of electricity.

"Not dangerous?!" Skylark leapt up again. "Amnesty says hundreds of people have been killed by Tasers!" He ran his hands through his hair. "Hey, what's going on with you, Corone? Boot camps, discipline, Tasers. Can it get any worse?"

"They only use them in emergencies," Corone defended himself.

For a moment I was so angry I almost wished I hadn't made a break for Corone's sake. But then I looked over at Kite and noticed her tired face, and I thought that I belonged with her and I didn't know why she was acting so totally strange toward me. Since we'd slept together I got the impression she'd walled herself up completely. Even her cell phone was turned off. I hardly dared look at her anymore, as if that was a crime or whatever. At least when Corone was around.

"Oh right, so Dipper was an emergency, was he?" I almost felt sorry for Skylark, 'cause he was making the effort of trying to argue with Corone's dumb ideas. "Pepper spray was only supposed to be used for defense originally too. But guys, it's Psychology 101: the inhibition level falls! They use pepper spray now even against peaceful blockades!"

Boy, was I tired. I mean, I hadn't just run. I hadn't just trained parkour. I'd been under a mighty amount of stress. Honest to God, I'd been scared.

"And you really didn't give them my coordinates?" asked Corone.

"No, we didn't tell them one word, about either of you," I heard Kite answer, quick as a flash.

Corone looked at Kite. Deadly serious. Everything around his mouth was hard as rock.

"If that's not true," he said quietly, "then it's really over between us, for good."

DIRTY LAUNDRY

Kite wanted to meet me.

At first I thought there was nobody there when I got to the old trade fair hall. Just the pigeons again, cooing beneath the roof and beating their wings. A couple feathers sailed down in front of me. It smelt odd, a mix of mold and fish and rain. I heard my footsteps echo as I walked over to the mattresses and threw down my backpack.

"Hey," came her voice from one side.

She stepped out of a dark corner, like she'd been hiding there.

"Hello," I said, and it sounded like nothing.

I was still feeling empty for some reason.

"Wanna sit down?" she asked.

I nodded and we crouched down. There was so much space between us, you coulda lined up at least ten origami crabs there.

"So what's up?" I asked, noticing that I didn't sound exactly gentleman-like. I looked over at some wreck of a machine, leaning totally rusty against one wall.

"I wanted you to know what's going on right now between Corone and me. It must all seem pretty strange to you," she said.

"Strange isn't the word I'd use."

"OK, Dipper, listen. There's nothing going on between Corone and me. The whole thing's over."

She put her hand on my arm. I brushed it off, like a big fat crumb. I suddenly realized how totally shitty it had all been for me. How much she'd hurt me.

"He's in trouble," she said. "I've been saying all along there was something funny about Corone's place, remember?"

I didn't answer.

"His mother hasn't been home in three months. She just went to work one day and never came back. He found an envelope of money from her in the mailbox, twice. But now even that's stopped."

I looked at Kite. What was she telling me here? It certainly didn't sound like some fairy story to worm her way out of things.

"You really saved his ass when you distracted the police," she said.

"What if something's happened to his mother?" I asked. "Maybe he should go to the police!"

Kite laughed out loud. "Happened? She's got a new lover, Corone told me that six months ago. He was supposed to be different to all the others, she said he had money and might buy a house for them all to live in."

"Does he even know about Corone and Kittiwake?"

"No way! I bet she's pretending she hasn't got kids. Some men don't like women with family baggage."

Woah there. It all started to fall into place.

"So that's why Corone never wanted you or the Urbans to go to his place?" I asked.

"I guess so." She looked at me and I looked at her. "They cut off the water and power about three weeks ago."

It went click again: Corone's old-man stink.

"I just wanted to tell you he's staying with me for a while. And Kittiwake too. You wouldn't believe how much laundry they put in my washing machine! The line in my apartment's full of clothes now, not origami."

"So what now?" I asked her.

Kite raised her shoulders to her ears and dropped them again in a huge shrug.

"Corone's waiting to hear from his mother. He checks the mailbox for another letter every day. He can't go to the police—don't you get it? He's not eighteen yet, they'd put him in a home for sure! The same with Kittiwake. And his mother'd end up in jail."

"Have you told him you're a traceuse?"

She pulled a face. "Hey, I can't do that to him right now, can I? He's got enough stress going on as it is. I just want to help him. It's real tough when you have to do everything on your own. I know that feeling."

Kite was really making herself small in front of Corone. I didn't like it. She was real clever and everything. I took a deep breath and then exhaled longer than you can imagine. I sounded like my ma after a twelve-hour day at the restroom paradise.

"Oh boy," I said. "That's the least funny news I've heard in a long time."

Kite nodded. "Tell me about it. And it's an organizational nightmare too. I have to go to class and Corone's busy as well. I guess parkour's real important for him right now. He

watches videos on the net until three or four in the morning, posts comments in this community, and he can't even
walk along the road without jumping over something." She
rubbed her eyes. "Whatever. We can't babysit for Kittiwake
around the clock, right? I'm pretty grateful that Professor
Bigshot, like you call him, is kind enough to look after her.
Yesterday they went to see the organ in Saint Peter's church.
Kittiwake was totally impressed. Pretty nice of him, huh?"
She smiled. "But he doesn't know any of what I've just told
you. You gotta swear you won't tell anyone, Dipper!"

She looked at me, begging me like you wouldn't believe
it.

"I promise," I said, nodding slowly. "You can count on
me."

Another secret I shared with Kite.

Boy, back then I really thought it was the right thing
to do. I mean, who'd rat on their own mother? And then
end up in a fucking home? No dude on this whole planet.
And it's not like going to the police ever gets you anywhere,
either. I swear, it either backfires on you or they send you
away and say: Come back when it's urgent. Come back once
Mr. X has punched you in the face, then we can do something for you. Thanks for that awesome support, guys. Been
there, done that. And my ma too.

"And you think Kittiwake won't tell?" I asked.

"She's keeping tight as a drum."

I looked over at the rusty old machine.

After a while of just sitting there in silence together, I
asked, "What's with your paper figures?"

"I don't have the space right now to make any new
ones," she said. "Maybe I'll take some paper to school and

fold something there." She looked at me. "You know what's my absolute dream?"

I shook my head.

"I wanna go to the Pacific Coast Origami Conference in Vancouver. I might even meet Robert Lang. Or Joseph Wu—he's the only person in the world who makes a living out of origami."

Suddenly, Kite sounded totally different than a moment ago. She was beaming with joy.

"Sounds pretty cool," I said, and I couldn't help smiling because she was so happy and all that. "Maybe I'll come along."

Oops. I hadn't meant to say that out loud.

"Oh, Dipper," she said quietly. "Sometimes everything's just so damn dark, huh?"

We got up. She leaned against me. We just stood like that for a while. At some point I saw two tears trickling down her face. I wiped them away with my finger.

"I feel so good with you," she whispered.

I kissed her where the tears had been.

"You wanna go training for an hour or so? Just you and me?" I asked her quietly.

"I'd love to."

We kissed again, this time properly. I nearly fainted when our tongues touched. I had goose bumps outside and inside. After a while Kite looked at me, and picked a couple of lint balls from my jacket.

That was totally cute.

"I'll help you," I said again. "Just let me know if you need me."

YOU GUYS ARE FUN / YOUR EYES TREAT ME LIKE A GUN

It had been ages since we'd met anywhere else but the park or the stadium or the old trade fair hall. We were really outside almost all the time. Before, Sky in particular had spent his whole life in front of his computer, playing WoW or something. I mean, Skylark's a genius at it, you need a whole lotta brain clarity to get to level 60. But still, at some point it threw him off his stride, you know? Once I was walking along next to him, he'd been up playing all night and he kept making these totally odd movements along the road, like there were all these people he had to liquidate in passing. Pretty weird stuff.

But that was before parkour.

Anyway, Jay had the idea of going to a concert. There was an American singer-songwriter playing at the Palas. Corone said he couldn't come because he had to look after Kittiwake. The usual. He said it was embarrassing to keep offloading his sister on Professor Bigshot and all that. No one knew he was staying with Kite except me, and I didn't say anything. Kite had left before Jay told us his idea. So it'd be just the three of us, and that was pretty cool by me. I really needed a break from all that on and off stuff. I mean, I'm not made of wood, you know?

Boy, it'd been so long since I last went out partying. I'd almost forgotten what to do. I had to truly strain my brain in front of my open closet to remember what to wear when you're out with people who aren't construction workers or traceurs.

Ma came in the door just as I was standing there in relatively clean jeans and a sweater, a totally unusual look for me.

"Going out, hon?" she asked.

"Yup." I gave her a kiss on the cheek.

She smelt of disinfectant.

I'll buy her some perfume for Christmas.

"You meeting that girl?" She hung up her scarf and took off her jacket.

"Nope," I said, and put on my bomber jacket. It's nothing to do with any of that sick Nazi stuff, I just think it's cool. "Boys' night out."

She pressed a five-euro bill into my palm. That was so sweet of her. You might get a glass of water for five euro at the Palas. But for Ma, it was a stack of money, I knew that.

"Take a look in the kitchen, there's something in there for you," I said, pocketing the cash. There was no sense turning the money down. Ma gets upset pretty quick about that kinda thing.

"Why, what is it?"

"See ya later!"

As I closed the door, I heard her call out in the kitchen.

"Hey, and mint green and all!"

She'd spotted the coffee maker.

On the way down to the front door, I did three passements and a demi-tour over the stair rail. My jeans were far too tight, dammit.

* * *

Skylark and I were standing outside the entrance to the Palas. It was cold as hell. I pulled my shoulders up.

"November sucks," I said.

Jay came round the corner. "Hey, guys!"

He was wearing clothes I'd never seen him in before. A pair of suit-pants like outta some old movie and a shirt. Over the top, a big black open coat with a big fat collar.

"Man, you're lookin' good!" said Skylark. "Real anachronistic."

Someone opened the doors at last, and everybody pushed and shoved toward the cash desk. I got a stamp pressed on my wrist.

"Come on, we can sit on these tables here," suggested Jay once we'd fought our way past the bar and the stage. We pushed the tables against the wall. "I'll get us some drinks. What do you guys want?"

"Beer," Skylark said.

And for me? "Vodka."

Skylark and I sat down and leaned back on the wall. The spot was dimly lit. More and more people were squeezing in. If you ask me, it's always awesome when people's glasses mist over. Looks totally strange. Some guy balanced a bar stool above people's heads. Next to us were two girls, stirring crushed ice in huge glasses with drinking straws. The

sound was real comforting. The voices blended into one…
I closed my eyes.

"Move up." Jay was standing in front of me, holding out
a vodka glass.

He squeezed in next to me.

We raised our glasses.

I knocked back the vodka in one slug. Boy, I hadn't
drunk vodka for so long. I could tell by the way it burned
like crazy in my throat. I pinched my eyes shut and shud-
dered.

"You'll be all right, kid," laughed Skylark, slapping me
on the back.

The girls next to us put their heads together and shot
a photo of themselves. I looked over at them. They were
both pretty cute actually; I guess I'd have been worked up a
couple weeks ago if they'd have sat next to me and stirred
their ice. But now I couldn't get Kite out of my brain. It was
just nice thinking about her, wherever I was. It made me real
happy. I slid off the table and went to get myself another
vodka. The problem is, you always drink it real fast, while
your buddies are still sucking at their beers for hours.

Some guys were fixing up mikes on stage. The air was
humid. There were crazy shadows on people's faces. One
couple stood close together, the girl leaning on her boy-
friend as he hugged her from behind.

"I'll have a vodka, please," I said to the guy behind the
bar.

I looked over at the love-drunk couple again. The guy
kept leaning down a little to his girl and kissing her on the
cheek or whispering who knows what in her ear. She smiled,

she looked totally happy. But he did too. For a moment I imagined Kite standing in front of me and me hugging her like that guy with his girlfriend. I took my vodka and just drank it at the bar; it was easiest like that. Next week, I thought, ordering another vodka-to-go in advance, next week I'll take Kite out to see a band or a movie. I was so glad she'd talked to me and I knew what was going on now. And that I didn't have to worry about anything anymore. That was really something to celebrate.

"Why the happy face, comrade?" Skylark asked me once I'd inserted myself between him and Jay on the table.

Luckily, something happened on stage right then.

"That's him," whispered Jay. "Simon Hersey."

Woah there, what kind of a freak was this? The singer guy sat down behind the mike, sporting a beard as long as your arm, glasses, and a three-foot-long knitted hat. I had to strain to look around someone standing in my way in a big jacket, with a beer in his hand.

"Thanks for being here, guys," said the freak, "I'm glad to be in this town. It's amazing." Someone whistled. "You guys are fun." He started playing.

"Hey, guys," said the guy in front of me at the same time.

"Man, Corone, cool," said Skylark.

Corone took off his jacket and unwound his scarf. "I did take Kittiwake to Professor Bigshot's place after all." He pulled a sheepish face. "I just really wanted to come."

My mood descended like an elevator. Not right down to the basement, let's say, but pretty much from the roof garden to the second floor. I took my vodka and tipped it down my throat. There was no burning anymore. And I wasn't dizzy or anything either. I was crystal clear. I swayed my legs. Everything totally relaxed. Corone was standing in my freakin' way. Just stay nice and calm, Dipper, I thought.

"Hey, over here, hey, your hopes, your fear," the hairy hat-man sang into the mike. Lyrics to change the world. He strummed at his guitar like crazy. Red light over the whole place.

Jay nodded his head in time, Skylark tapped out the beat. I saw the music through a visualizer on a laptop at the mixing desk. Green jagged lines snaked across the screen, beautiful. Like an ECG of the sound. The air was even more humid than just a moment before. The music got louder. There was a lamp hanging from the ceiling by our table, and someone kept banging their head against it. Once the light bulbs went out, and at the next bump they went back on again. Kinda funny. I giggled like I was sitting in the kitchen with my ma at three thirty in the morning.

"Well, look who's here," said Skylark. "Our traceuse-in-training's made it along too."

My heart beat out a spontaneous tattoo before I'd even seen her.

"Hey, Kite! Now the Urban Planetbirds are out in full strength," said a cheerful Jay.

That relaxed feeling I'd had took an instant wipeout. Kite shrugged her bag off her shoulder and took off her jacket. Underneath, she was wearing a miniskirt, pantyhose, and boots. She looked so sexy I had to face the other direction to get my already racing pulse to slow down. Right next to me was a fire extinguisher on the wall, and I thought: you're my savior. I really thought that crap. The only funny thing was that Kite didn't come over to me this time, either.

She stood next to Corone instead. But there wasn't much space where we were, anyway, I thought. Maybe that's why.

The freak had just finished a song and the audience was clapping and cheering. He started talking crap again. His whole mellow chat thing was getting annoying. All over the place, cell phone or camera displays lit up in the semi-darkness. I saw hands folded over beer bottles clenched to bellies, girls chewing gum, people sitting on the floor, and the couple from before, now hugging tightly, too tightly, I thought, and swaying to the rhythm of the next song, which the hairy hat-man had just kicked off. I watched from behind as Kite talked to Corone. I wondered why she hadn't come over to say hello to me yet, or kiss me, or whatever. The whole crowd was singing along. The hairy hat-man fired them on with his bedroom voice. I didn't sing, not one note. But Jay was singing. He didn't even notice that the guy up there was an arrogant little rat. Kite and Corone were standing so close their arms touched. I didn't think it was so crowded that they really had to get that close. And suddenly I had a total vision: I saw light between the two of them, orange and red light, right where their arms brushed against each other. I swear I really saw it: right there in between all those people in the dark.

"Fuck!" I rubbed my eyes.

"Shhh!" said Jay.

"Your eyes treat me like a gun," everyone whispered along with the hairy hat-man, and at that moment Kite turned around to us and smiled. Then she whispered something in Corone's ear. He had his hands in his pockets and he was moving his legs to the beat. He laughed, and the two of them looked up at the stage again.

I grabbed Skylark's beer bottle and drained it dry.

"Hey!" he hissed, holding the empty bottle up to a dim light bulb, angry, and then in front of my face. "What are you playing at?"

Man, had I had enough of that dumb wailer up on stage.

"I can't wait to see your préci tomorrow," Sky carried on, waving the bottle around in front of me.

By the time he put it down at last, Corone and Kite had disappeared. Really disappeared, like the ground had swallowed them up. I strained my neck and searched the room, as far as I could. But it was so damn overcrowded there was no point. The hairy hat-man was scrubbing away louder and louder at his guitar. The ECG went off the screen. Then, when the freak collapsed over his instrument in pseudo-exhaustion, the green jags on the screen sank to the bottom like snowflakes.

Then hands in the air everywhere, camera flashes. I didn't join in the applause. Got up, pushed my way past all the pathetic, enthusiastic idiots, and went looking for Kite.

Sometimes you can see something coming and you wish it was just your stupid imagination and everything's just fine and normal and all that. But it wasn't.

When I got outside I saw Corone and Kite. I stood still as a statue. Stared at them. Their faces like one face. Corone's hands in Kite's hair. They were kissing. And not like a brother and sister.

NO-ZONE

The next night, I called Jay.

"Hey, where did you get to all of a sudden last night?" he asked. "Did you hate the singer so bad you had to leave?"

"No." I laughed, even though that was the last thing I felt like. "I just wanted to let you know I can't come for a week. I'm on a new construction site. Tons of work there, I can't make it in the afternoons."

"Shame," answered Jay. "You think it'll be OK again after that?"

"Maybe," I mumbled.

"Jeez, I'm glad of every hour I can get away from here and go training," said Jay.

"Is Professor Bigshot so bad right now, or what?"

"Oh, I don't know. I'm almost only here to sleep, or I creep to the icebox or the bathroom. I just ignore the rest of the house completely, including my father. And anyway, he's got Kittiwake now, his new adopted daughter. She's a wonderful distraction for him."

"I've heard of cooler roommates," I said.

"You sound so depressed," said Jay. "Everything OK?"

"Everything's fine." I made an effort not to sound as rough as I felt.

"Come back soon, OK? The Urbans aren't complete without you."

"Sure, see ya soon. Keep on running."

Then I dialed Skylark's number.

"That's just the point. That's why I'm in favor of a basic income for all, man," he started in after I explained the situation. "It sucks that you have to work your ass off, hardly earning anything, and you don't even have enough spare time to do what you want! It makes me wanna hurl!"

Sky was always so awesome at getting agitated.

"So how did you like the gig, anyway?" I tried to distract him from any further political discussion.

"I'll tell you what I think of that guy," said Skylark. "He wasn't into WoW, he was one of those kids who goes for simulations. I guess he dug agriculture simulation—plowing, sowing, harvesting, selling, you know."

Now I did have to laugh. Hard.

"Oh well, he didn't do anyone any harm," said Skylark once I'd stopped pissing my pants. "And how did you like it?"

"He wasn't exactly Eminem's little brother," I answered.

It's a funny feeling, laughing when you've got the world's blackest lump of tar perched on your solar plexus. Kinda like breathing under a sack of cement.

"Well, I'll be thinking of you at my next demo for basic incomes," Skylark added. "See ya, Dipper."

I hung up.

I fetched the crumpled origami paper out of my backpack and stuffed it in the trash.

The next day, I went to the doctor and got a sick note.

* * *

I'd discovered a corner of the park that was ideal: far enough away from the Urban Planetbirds' spots and far enough away from my work. I left the house in the morning as if I was going to work, got changed in the park, and started training. I kicked off with jumping jacks, burpees, bootstrappers. Then came push-ups and lunges, Hindu squats, animal walks, smaller drops. After that I jogged for a half hour with short sprints in between, before I finally began training basic parkour moves. I repeated and practiced, practiced and repeated. In my backpack was fruit and water, nothing else. When I found a couple scraps of that dumb origami paper, I crumpled it up and threw it in the nearest trashcan, disgusted.

Five days in, I started training jumps I'd never done before. Maybe because I didn't have to think about the basics anymore. The spooky thing was, I couldn't stop. I guess I spent ten hours outdoors every day. At night I dreamed about the moves.

I was real worried I might punch Corone in the face at the next opportunity. OK, I coulda worn myself out at work, but I had no idea how I coulda put up with my workmates' permanent dumb comments, what with that freakin' black lump of tar on my solar plexus.

I needed to be alone.

And I needed to fight.

With myself.

One thing was for sure, at least: if my heart was beating, it was mine, dammit.

* * *

My secret training spot seemed to be cut off from anyone else. I swear I didn't see a single person for six days. So I was real confused on the seventh day, right after a double chat over a moss-coated Ping-Pong table, to see someone coming toward me. My spot was a little way up from the river; you had to climb a broken old staircase to reach it. The man walking up to me was short, with thick black hair. As he came closer I saw he was Asian. I leaned against the tabletop and reached into my backpack for water.

This is my no-zone, I thought. Don't you disturb, Mister.

"Hello," said Mister, nodding two or three times, probably in case I hadn't noticed his first nod.

He pointed at a stone bollard.

I gave a silent nod and he sat down. There's always a whole load o' crazies in the park, so I wasn't the friendly and open type straight away. And there were gay cruisers too.

I drank my water.

"It's very interesting, what you're showing," the guy said in stilted German.

"I'm not showing anything." My voice sounded totally unfamiliar because I'd hardly talked to anyone for days. "I'm training."

"Do you understand English?" the man asked now. "My spoken German is not that fluent."

I nodded.

"I've been watching you for quite a long time now," he said, "and I saw your battle."

I drank more water, watching him.

Was this something outta some samurai movie, where I'd have to pass a test in combat?

"I don't know what your inner battle is all about, but let me tell you something: learn more from the inside of your mind. What you're doing here is a metaphor for life."

He looked me straight in the eye—he wasn't faking, there was no spark of arrogance. I looked back, and everything between us was in balance.

"Tell me what you love about this way of movement, will you?"

I put the bottle back in my backpack and said: "What I'm training here is parkour. You can use it anywhere, anytime. You don't need anything except your body. It's like music without instruments, do you understand?"

The man smiled, and a whole web of lines shone out around his eyes.

"Like singing with muscles and bones?"

"Yes," I answered. "And it's good because you can use it to help people or rescue them in an emergency. And you can get away real quick too, if you want to." I grinned.

"It seems to me as though you are trying to move in complete harmony with the environment."

"Cities are full of boundaries," I said. "We could break them, those boundaries, spray them, or blast ourselves into space so we don't notice them anymore. But it's cooler to get over them with your own power. Everything else is frustrating and doesn't change anything. When I'm doing parkour, nothing about my surroundings changes either, but my view of them does change a whole lot."

"It's all about choice." He nodded. "Listen, you train to overcome obstacles with your body. But what you train here is also perfect for getting used to overcoming fear and so-called barriers; you can't solve everything by training body-movements. In the end, you have to transfer it to your every-day life."

An image flashed across my mind. One I'd stopped myself from thinking of for days. Kite.

Was I running away from her?

From Corone?

Had I been lying to myself here for days?

Then it went quiet. Inside me. Between the visitor and me. I can't say how long it lasted. A second. Days. It was as if I was together with everybody, everywhere, and at the same time alone under a glass bell jar.

Then, out of the blue, came a clear thought:

I'm not running away.

And another one:

I'm preparing myself, my muscles, my bones.

And suddenly I knew:

Kite wasn't the problem here.

My visitor got up.

"It was nice to meet you, Dipper. Don't you stop developing. Keep on moving."

He smiled, turned around, and walked down the steps toward the river.

* * *

I woke up as my alarm clock bleeped without mercy. A Friday in November, five thirty in the morning, still pitch black outside. The coffee maker was producing the ultimate new sound of home in the kitchen.

"Better watch out, out there today," said Ma when I walked in the room. "Might be an unlucky day, you know, Friday the thirteenth and all that."

"And good morning to you too."

She poured coffee in my cup and sat down opposite me.

"You're looking good. Hardly seen you all last week. You've slimmed down. And you got muscles."

"Really?"

Ma nodded. I sure felt pretty good—the lump of tar was only half the original size—but I didn't know you could tell by looking.

"That's love, that is, making you look so good," said Ma.

Tell me about it.

I didn't break a leg that Friday the thirteenth, but when I got to work they told me we were being sent to a site four hundred miles away. For two whole weeks. We'd be staying in trailers, but the pay was great. I said I'd do it.

SEEING RED

"Man, it's about time we got back, I've got a hard-on this long! My old lady's lookin' forward to seeing me," said my workmate once we returned two weeks later.

It was almost time to knock off, and the three of us were sitting in a supermarket café, right by the cash desks. Three mugs of coffee on the table.

I didn't comment.

"I wouldn't push her out of bed either." My other work-mate gestured with his chin at the waitress, who was reaching up to a shelf, revealing a phat tattoo above the back of her apron. He ran one hand over his bald head. He was definitely easier to get along with than the other guy, but I'd got used to both of them—we'd been stuffed in the trailer like sardines. Baldie grinned and tried to give the waitress some totally dumb signs that he thought she was sexy or whatever. She tapped a finger to her forehead, and I looked under the table. Our shoes were so encrusted with dirt that I couldn't say what color they were underneath. I was glad as hell to be back. I hadn't had enough time for parkour since my week of extreme training, but I'd sure been building up my strength.

"Hey, buddy!" my workmate with the hair hissed suddenly. "Look at that little hottie over there!" He turned to the storefront window, which had a view of the street corner. Baldie and I turned round as well.

At first all I saw was some messed-up guy in giant sneakers standing at the stoplight. He conducted the car turning in front of him with a grand gesture, then the next one and the next one. At last he hobbled away, looking like that was his mega-performance of the day. Poor loser, I thought—your best days are over, dude.

What I saw next was a slap in the face for me.

A slap with the back of a hand.

I stared at the girl teetering past out there.

"Isn't that kid a total babe? Look at that hot miniskirt! And the boots with it! Lolita, honey, c'mere, I'll show you something real sweet!"

He clicked his tongue and swallowed.

I got up, walked round the table, and punched him in the mouth. There was a kinda crunching sound. It went dead silent all around us. Even the constant beeping of the scanners at the cash desks stopped. Everyone stared over at us.

My workmate held his hands in front of his face. Blood seeped between his fingers, dripping onto the packs of sugar on the table. The paper and sugar absorbed the blood, turning pink." Suddenly, as if someone had switched the supermarket café world back on again, all these people ran over to help him.

Strangely enough, no one took any notice of me.

I turned round and walked real slowly out of the glass doors onto the street.

I saw her about a hundred yards away.

"Kittiwake!" I yelled. "Kittiwake! Wait!"

"Dipper, Dipper, Dipper!" screamed Kittiwake.

She threw her arms round me and almost squeezed me to death.

"Hey kiddo, haven't seen you for weeks," I said, looking at her. "Where'd you get the lipstick?"

She'd painted her mouth red.

"From Mom," said Kittiwake.

"Are you allowed to just take it?"

"Mmm-hm."

She gave an eager nod and then looked away. She was real restless. It was only now I noticed the white iPod round her neck. It was dark, only the street lamps dribbling a joyless trickle of light over the heads of the people running round out there. And it wasn't exactly warm either.

"Where you going?" I asked.

Kittiwake shrugged.

She's ten years old, I thought.

"Jay's pa don't have time today." She frowned. "Not going there till tomorrow."

She sniffed and put her red hands in her jacket pockets. I took a careful look at her. At least she had pantyhose on under that tiny skirt.

"You cold?"

She shook her head.

"Why don't you come to our place," I said. "I bet my ma'd be pleased to see you again. Wanna come?"

She grinned. "Dipper-Ma, yay!"

She started skipping on the way.

"So whatta you got on your mega-cool iPod then?"

Two dogs panted past us, wearing neon-green collars that flashed in the dark.

"Hey look, Christmas dogs," said Kittiwake.

She watched the dogs for ages, and I had to give her a nudge after a while to remind her to keep walking. She'd forgotten my question of course, so I asked her again.

"Organ music from Jay's pa. He magicked it in there." She held the iPod out to me so I could see the magic too. "He gave it to me 'cause I'm a good girl."

"Cool."

At least there's one person looking out for Kittiwake, I thought. Her mother doesn't seem to care anymore.

We got to the weir not far from the first training spot. You could hear the water from at least two hundred yards away. Next to it was a retirement home, and I always thought they must all have a screw loose from having to listen to that crazy loud water all the time. It was really the least quiet weir you can ever imagine. Majorly unkind sound design.

"Who put that there?"

Kittiwake pointed at something.

She was standing in front of a wire fence next to the weir. Two red ribbons fluttered from it in the wind. On the ground was a teddy bear, a little stuffed bunny perched on its lap, both gray with dirt and rain, and all around them little red plastic cups with candles that had gone out. I knelt down and looked at the whole lot more closely.

"No idea. Guess a child fell in the water here and drowned."

Kittiwake ran onto the bridge over the weir and tried to look down at the river over the thick wall.

"Can you lift me up?" she asked, and I stood behind her and lifted her so that she could lean her stomach on the wall.

92

We stared down at the water, head to head. It shot down vertically for about ten feet, swirling into crazy foam at the bottom. It crashed so loudly you had to shout to make yourself understood. To the left and right of the waterfall were little huts with tiled roofs. There was a sign on one of them:

"Danger of death! Beware of high water."

Tell me about it, I thought. I wanted to get Kittiwake outta there real quick, so I lifted her back down to the ground.

"This is where you end up when you tell tales," she said. "Then you fall down and water gets into you everywhere and then you're dead."

"Bull. Who told you that?"

"No one, I just know it on my own," Kittiwake said quickly. "C'mon, we'd better run away!"

She ran off and I ran after her. For the first time in two weeks, I jumped over a couple obstacles.

Woah there, I was back home!

And parkour was waiting for me.

I had to call Corone so he knew where his sister was, even though that was tough. But I hadn't been fighting for nothing. Before I dialed his number, I loosened up as much as possible and did a couple practice grins.

"Hey," I said when he picked up, "I got your sister here. If you wanna see her alive, leave 250,000 euros in small bills in the trashcan at the Mercado restroom paradise."

"Jeez!" he yelled. "Kittiwake's at your place? I thought she was at her after-school club!"

"Corone, it's after seven—even dipshit schools close by then."

I heard a rustling sound.

"Seven already? Fuck! Kite, I gotta go!"

A faint stab, somewhere between my stomach and my heart. Maybe because the lump of tar was gone now, I thought. Before my mind's eye I saw Kite's large room, the origami shapes, the sofa bed, folded out, with crumpled sheets.

"I'll come get her in twenty minutes."

I hung up and went in the kitchen.

"I'm winning again," sighed Kittiwake. "Dipper-Ma's lost four times already." She frowned and eyed my ma. "Are you sad now?"

Ma hid her face in her hands and acted like she was just gonna break out crying. Kittiwake stared at her, shocked. Then Ma raised her head and laughed.

"No, sweetpea, I'm not sad, I'm just kidding. It's just a game! You don't need to get sad about games ever in your life, you hear?"

"Crying's not allowed." Kittiwake picked up a piece and leapt right across the board with it, until she reached my ma's triangle. "Playing games is fun, that's all, it's not sad, and you don't need to be scared neither."

"That's right," laughed Ma.

They were a real cool team, my ma and Kittiwake and the Halma board. I coulda watched them and listened to them for hours. But not much later, there was a ring at the door.

Kittiwake looked at me, kinda urgently or something. "Can I stay here?"

"You mean sleep over?" I asked.

"Live here," she murmured, her head drooping as I went down the hall and opened the door.

A cold-ass wind came blowing in. Corone held his hand out to me. We tapped fists.

"You wanna come in?" I couldn't look him in the face.

"No thanks, I totally lost track of time. My mother'll be mad if I get back so late with the kiddo."

I felt bad that I knew. That I knew Corone was lying.

"Kittiwake!" he called over my shoulder, adding quietly, "Thanks for babysitting, won't happen again."

Kittiwake came trotting out of the kitchen.

"Will I see you at training tomorrow?" Corone put a ciggie between his lips.

"You better believe it," I said.

Ma poked her head round the kitchen door.

"Say hi to your mother, and tell her not to let your sister wear skirts like that in this weather!"

Corone's eyes flickered to one side just for a moment, then he looked over at Ma again. "I'll tell her."

Kittiwake didn't say anything. Not even goodbye. She took Corone's outstretched hand and walked along the corridor next to him, silent.

"That kid'll catch her death in them clothes," Ma cursed, and I heard her sliding the Halma pieces into the box in the kitchen.

* * *

I have no idea how long the hot water splashed over the back of my neck that evening. Certainly longer than it's actually allowed in Dipper-Ma's household. But Ma had gone over to a neighbor, so she couldn't drum at the bathroom door like an African queen as she usually did when she thought I was wasting hot water.

Steam quivered all around me. My skin was pretty red by now. I felt like I had to wash everything off. Everything that had happened over the last few days and weeks. And I had to have a good long think. How did you do that anyway— a good long think? I certainly never managed it whenever I meant to. My thoughts kept dodging off. Right now, for example, I was thinking I'd go put a frozen pizza in the stove in a minute. That I hadn't watched TV for weeks. I thought of Kite. I thought about running away from the cops. All of a sudden I remembered the horror dream I'd had about Kittiwake not long ago.

I turned off the shower, took my towel off the door handle and dried myself off. I could see myself down to my hips in the mirror. I was in pretty good shape now. I mean, I didn't look like some huge bodybuilder, but they look pretty dumb to me anyway. This was just the result of natural moves. My body had strength and you could tell.

Maybe in my next nightmare I'd make it: saut de détente onto the next roof and save Kittiwake from the evil crow.

I switched on my father's shaver and ploughed it across my chin. About once a week was all it took; good old Dipper didn't have much beard going on yet. I secretly thought that if I kept on shaving I'd get more of a beard growing. It was pretty awesome that my Pa's shaver had survived so long and was still buzzing away.

As I rinsed out the washbowl, I imagined what it'd be like if the water suddenly stopped coming out of the faucet. And as I sat in the living room waiting for my pizza, I thought what it'd be like without the stove, without the TV set that I switched on.

I tried to think it all out real precisely, but to be honest, man, I couldn't imagine it at all. I was pretty damn used to water coming out of the faucet, hot and cold, and to it being light, even at night and in the winter. Somewhere in Outer Mongolia or whatever it must be different, but in Germany? At Corone's place?

Actually, Corone wasn't the one I felt sorry for. The guy'd be eighteen in two years' time and he could take care of his own life. But Kittiwake. I was getting more and more worried about her. She was a kid, and how can a kid understand that her ma's just staying away, and she's supposed to keep as silent as a grave about it and all? Kittiwake was getting pushed around like some stupid, unwanted pet.

Boy, was I mad all of a sudden. All that thinking's no good for me, I swear. It got me real nervous. I zapped from one channel to the next with the remote. I don't think I actually watched anything at all.

At some point there was a bad stink of burning. I ran in the kitchen. Tons of smoke everywhere. I yanked the stove door open and even more smoke streamed in my face. I coughed like tuberculosis. In the stove was a flat black circle of charcoal. Pizza Diabolo, mon amour. Ciao. That's what comes of all that thinking—I really don't recommend it. I tore open the kitchen window and took a deep breath.

Then I put on my jacket, left the apartment, and walked to the stadium in the dark.

* * *

I stood in front of the monster wall. Floodlights gleamed on my back; my shadow was crazy long.

My fortune awaited me behind that wall.

I breathed in.

Out.

Concentrated.

I breathed in again, out again.

Behind that wall…emptiness.

Then I took a run-up. Fast, faster. I didn't put on the brakes like usual when the wall got closer and closer. The wall wasn't a wall. It was a path. I jumped and pushed myself off with a large upward step. Grabbed the top edge. Held on tight. Pulled myself up with both arms. I had the strength; it was there. With momentum, I levered my left leg onto the wall and pulled the right one over the side.

Boy, was that awesome. It was so awesome.

Everything looked so different from up there. The street. The lights. And there was something else I'd never seen before: four stone pillars rose up ahead of me. A letter on each one. I read: L. O. S. T.

Then I looked down again from the wall, across the street. The city flickered all its lights in the distance like a huge portion of Christmas. The velvet sky above it all. It was kinda amazing. Not stuck in between the crowds like the mortar in cracks in the walls. Not locked away between all the stuff they've built up around us. Releasing yourself from it. Or melting into it. Or both at the same time. Is that even possible? Something like that went through my mind up there. I was real happy.

And I'd misread those pillars. I noticed it when I turned back toward them. They said something different. They said: L. O. V. E.

Suddenly, no idea why right that moment, I made a decision.

I wanted to let Jay in on the thing with Corone, Kite, and Kittiwake. Three weeks had passed since I'd found out about it all. And I felt bad about it. It wasn't just about Corone somehow. Or about him and Kite and me.

Something about the whole thing was pretty damn odd.

I just didn't know what it was yet.

FIRST SMILES

"Pardon?" Jay sounded horrified. "Their mother's disappeared?!"

Lying on my bed, I swapped the telephone from one ear to the other.

"You can't really say she's disappeared. She's with her new lover or something, Kite says. Corone's waiting for her to get in touch and send money."

There was a crashing sound. Jay'd probably dropped down onto a chair. Now that I'd told someone the whole thing it seemed totally bad, much worse than I'd been thinking the whole time.

"What d'you think?" I asked. "Can your father get it sorted out? He knows about that kinda stuff, right?"

Jay snorted.

"Sort it out? What does that mean? He's a lawyer, sure. We can ask him if Corone and Kittiwake stand a chance of not getting put in a home, and if their mother stands a chance of not getting put in jail for child neglect."

I didn't reply.

"Boy, this is pretty drastic," said Jay.

"Sure, I realize that."

Neither of us said anything. For at least a minute. That's always totally strange on the telephone. You're holding the receiver to your ear and nothing comes out.

"It's all about Kittiwake," I said at some point. "It's all about her."

It had suddenly dawned on me.

"Yeah," said Jay, and then: "Come over, Dipper. My father's home. I don't think we should wait any longer."

* * *

Professor Bigshot's face was a picture when Jay asked if we could talk to him. He looked at least as suspicious as Jay usually did when his father wanted something from him. But it wasn't about them this time. And anyway, Professor Bigshot was the only adult for miles around who'd taken care of Kittiwake in the past few weeks.

"Take a seat," he said, and I felt like I was at some job interview or whatever.

Professor Bigshot sat down on his white leather armchair. He was wearing leather slippers with socks.

"So what's this all about?" he probed when I didn't say anything, and Jay didn't either.

He seemed nervous. Like we were just about to punch him or something.

"Dipper, you tell him," said Jay.

And I did.

Professor Bigshot listened, I had to give him that. He didn't interrupt me once. I mean, OK—it wasn't like when my ma listens to me at three thirty in the morning, with nods and raised eyebrows and all that, but still. I'd thought he might go crazy when we told him what was up with Kittiwake and Corone, but he was different. Something in his face seemed to smooth out, I guess. He looked almost relaxed.

"And now we're wondering," Jay took over from me, "if Corone and Kittiwake really have to go to a home and their mother would end up in jail if we went to the police."

Jay's father stood up and massaged the spot where his mustache would be if he had one. Then he started pacing to and fro, watching the tips of his slippers like pets walking obediently at heel.

"I blame myself," he said in the end, coming to a standstill.

"You?" It just slipped out. "Why?"

He nodded and started pacing again.

"Why didn't I notice anything?" he asked us, or himself, I don't know which. "She's been here so often. I should have noticed something! And why didn't she tell me?"

He shook his head, and I really thought, man, he really cares. He's really upset—Professor Bigshot, the guy who always has to have everything under control.

"Well, Kittiwake's not supposed to tell tales," I tried to console him. "She's been primed not to tell."

"And she doesn't know you well enough to trust you with the truth," Jay added.

Professor Bigshot sat back down on his leather seat, resting his head in his hands. Jay and I exchanged a brief glance. We were waiting for some kind of inspiration, some damn words that would help us.

"You know, family law's not my specialty," he said, raising his head. "But I'll check. Of course. I'll get onto it first thing in the morning. I'll let you know right away as soon as I can say anything for sure, so we can take action. It might take me a few days though, I have an important appointment this week. Is that all right?"

Boy, it wasn't exactly a magic spell from Gandalf the Gray, but this was real life. Have patience and all that. At least, that's what I thought.

"Sure," I said. "Thanks for your help."

"Yeah, thanks, Dad," Jay smiled.

Professor Bigshot smiled back.

I bet that was the first smile the two of them exchanged in about the last thousand years.

IN MIDAIR

We were up in midair. First, because we had to wait for Professor Bigshot to find out enough about the laws, and then physically too. Skylark had come across the coolest-ever move on the net, and he wanted to teach us it.

It was ice-cold that day, sunny and dry. A crazy pattern of condensation lines in the sky, and you could make out the planes at the start of the thinner lines, minuscule and shiny. All the Urbans were there, even Kittiwake. She was wearing a thick flower-patterned quilted jacket, pants and boots, a scarf, gloves, and a hat.

"Jay's father took her out shopping yesterday. Doesn't she look cute?" Kite whispered, so close to me that I could smell her. And she smelled damn good, of moisturizer and all that. But still. I'd had enough of all this whispering and passing notes and that kinda crap. We weren't at elementary school anymore. Did she think I'd keep on being her buddy and her shoulder to cry on, the guy she could just make out with whenever she felt lonely? Some guy she never kissed in front of the others? I'd had it up to here. I just nodded, concentrating on what Sky was showing us.

"It looks like it's majorly difficult, but it's zero complicated. I'll show you how it goes."

He sat down backward on the edge of the wall, behind it an eight or nine-foot drop to a flowerbed.

"Put your backside a hand's width away from the edge," he said, sliding away. "Grab the edge with your hands on the left and right, elbows back. Then bend your upper body back over the edge, pull your legs over your head. And let go!"

Sky somersaulted backward and dropped to the ground. He landed on two feet in the flowerbed.

"Easy," he called up at us, as we all looked down at him like chickens in a coop.

"Cool," I said.

"Correct," said Corone. "It's about time we learned something new round here!"

"It's a roly-poly, but backward and down," Kittiwake thought out loud.

I glanced at her, glad to see her looking just like a normal child, without lipstick and short skirts. She was still pale and thin as a rake. You could still tell that, even though she was wrapped up in so much padding. It sure was time something happened.

"Awesome!" said Corone, who was just coming back in a passe muraille. "We'll all practice it one at a time, thirty times over, so we get it just perfect. C'mon, line 'em up!"

We started training, and we all tried not to notice Corone ordering us around. Because this move was a whole lotta fun. There's something about rotating round your own axis. It's like you're saying, hey, you can do things differently. I mean, that sounds like something outta the world's dumbest fortune cookie, but just think about it for a second. You can do things differently. It's actually totally dope.

While I waited my turn, breathing white clouds into the icy air, I looked into the bare tops of the trees around us.

The branches were covered in crows, the sun shining like a gold ball behind them.

Then I looked at us, the Urban Planetbirds. I thought: Kite knows that I know what she and Corone and Kittiwake know, but Corone and Kittiwake don't know it. I know that Jay knows what I know, but Corone and Kite and Kittiwake don't know it. Professor Bigshot knows what Jay and I know, but nobody else knows it. And Skylark doesn't know anything. Woah there. All these big secrets weren't my thing. I felt like a fake Dipper. Dishonest. The spider's threads had become a sticky web, without us even noticing. What if we just spoke openly to Corone and the others, and all of us knew what was going on here?

"Oh boy, honey, you're not exactly a natural at parkour, are you?" Corone was saying, laughing his ass off at Kite, who was lying down in the flowerbed, rubbing her side and groaning.

The problem was that Corone hadn't stopped making those dumb comments of his recently, and I was having major problems still seeing him as my friend.

"Dipper, wakey wakey!" Corone yelled in my ear right then. It was my turn, and I hadn't noticed.

I sat down on the wall, grabbed the edge with my hands and rolled over backward. As I fell, I knew I wanted to put my cards on the table.

The Urban Planetbirds belonged together, and I wasn't gonna let this thing break us up.

As I landed and looked up, the first snowflakes fell.

DEAL

One afternoon later, I was staring at the corner of the room where the fat Asian guy was hanging on the wall. Sure, it was tough what Corone had to deal with, but he'd just have to take it, I thought once we laid the cards on the table. It was so damn quiet, we'd probably all have died of a mass heart attack if a flea had sneezed. Apart from Skylark, who was out marching some street or other in favor of basic income, and Kittiwake, who was at her after-school club, we were all gathered together in Jay's room.

Corone was trembling all over. I could see every breath he took, and I could tell damn well he was finding it hard to breathe.

"You guys—you've betrayed me."

The worst thing was the way he said it. Too quietly. He was quaking, his whole body was trembling. Jay, Kite, and I exchanged glances. Corone had been staring at the nasty old patterned carpet the whole time. Jesus H. Christ. Something was ticking away here like a bomb just about to explode.

"Corone," Jay started in, "we just wanted…"

One second later, Corone had pushed Jay onto the bed and pressed his arm right across his throat.

"You shut your measly little mouth, you asshole! Don't you dare ever say one word to me again, never again, you hear me?"

I got up and stepped slowly behind Corone, when I heard a click. I knew that sound—I stopped in my tracks.

"And if you go running to the cops I'll slit your throat, you get it?"

I saw the blade close up against Jay's neck.

"You get it, asshole?"

"Yes," was Jay's quiet answer.

Corone pressed Jay against the mattress one more time and then turned round to me, the knife in his hand.

"And the same goes for you, you loser," he hissed. To Kite, he said, "And you? You're just a lying piece of shit!"

He threw something in her direction. I broke out in an instant sweat. But Kite bent down, and I saw that Corone had thrown a key at her feet.

"You're never gonna see me again."

He yanked open the door and ran down the stairs.

Kite collapsed on the carpet and started crying.

Jay gave me a silent signal and we crept out in the hall. We heard voices from downstairs.

"Shut up!" yelled Corone. "And I'll tell you one thing: You keep away from my sister, you uptight pervert!"

"But I…"

We heard Corone again, this time quieter and more threatening:

"One word to the cops about my family, and I'll tell them something too. Like about how you've got a dirty deal going with my sister, for instance. How about that, huh? They'd love to hear something like that, you can bet your life!"

A second later, the front door slammed so hard that the stair rail shook all the way to the top. The next moment,

Kite came running past us, down the stairs and out the front door.

Then it was as silent as a grave.

Until I asked:

"Deal? What kind of a deal?"

Professor Bigshot raised his head and saw us at the top of the stairs.

"What are you doing up there?"

It didn't sound all that friendly.

"I live here, in case you've forgotten," said Jay.

"Don't you get fresh with me, Sebastian!"

"What was the deal Corone was talking about, Father?"

Professor Bigshot took a step to the left, then to the right, like he'd forgotten something or whatever.

"Oh, the boy's got a sick imagination!" He went to the door. It was only then I noticed he was pulling along a little suitcase on wheels. "I have to go, my plane takes off in an hour." Something in his face was totally twisted, contorted, as he looked up at us again. "There'll be consequences—I don't care whether your friend ends up in a home or his mother in prison, I'll tell you that right now."

He dragged the case out the door. An icy wind blew in.

The front door slammed for the third time.

* * *

What Jay did next was actually totally insane. I mean, it was his home and it's his father. And no matter what kind of asswipe your father is, he's still your father. Your flesh and blood. If he has some evil growth attacking his body, you feel it too.

We went through the entire damn house. We started in the basement, went up to the first floor, then the second, where Jay's and his father's rooms were. I swear I didn't have the slightest idea what we were looking for, and I guess Jay didn't know it either. We just looked at the whole house like we were strangers. As if it was the first time we'd been there. There was something about the way Jay was acting, like he was running a fever. His breathing was louder than usual and his eyes were scary—big and shiny.

To finish up with, he pushed open the door to the attic.

"What do you want up here?" I asked as he flicked on the light and walked across the floorboards. They creaked slightly like in some scary horror story.

Jay didn't answer. I followed his footsteps, slowly. The attic was cramped, the sloping roof almost touching the top of my head. And it was complete chaos. Woah there. Our section of attic at home looked a thousand times neater, I thought. Ma didn't want people to see anything up there that showed us up in a bad light. This place certainly showed Jay and his family up in a real mean light.

"Hey, didn't they say they were gonna clear this place out?" I asked.

Jay still didn't say anything.

It smelled pretty damn dusty, and suddenly I sneezed as hard as a hippo with a water allergy. My head flung itself downward. And then I saw something on the floor right in front of me. Really right by my feet. I bent down to pick it up.

"Look," I said, holding out a dirty gray toy bunny to Jay. He came closer.

I said, "Kittiwake and I saw this at the weir the other day. Some child must have drowned or something. How the hell did it get here?"

Jay still didn't say a word, I swear. He looked like he was on autopilot. He took the bunny out of my hand and stared at it. Then he dropped it, turned on his heel and walked over to this strange ladder at the back of the attic. It looked pretty damn instable.

"You wanna break your neck?" I asked, worried now.

"That's what my dad's always saying." His voice sounded like somebody else's. "That's why we were never allowed up here. He said if the trap door opened the whole roof would collapse on top of us."

He started climbing the rungs.

"Jesus, Jay, what if it's true?"

I was standing at the bottom of the ladder, holding onto it with both hands, as if that would stop the roof from collapsing.

Jay had made it to the trap door, drew in his head and back, and pressed against it. The door stayed put.

"He's padlocked it," he said in a strangely calm tone. "You can deal with that kind of thing, can't you, Dipper?"

I didn't ask why Jay thought I could "deal with that kind of thing." I just climbed up and damn well opened the lock.

The two of us pressed our shoulders against the trap door. A crack gaped, and we opened it all the way.

ICE FLOWERS

I still don't get it to this day. I can't. They can explain it a thousand times, on TV or whatever—I just don't get it. How it can happen. Fuck, I don't get it.

We were in a gable. Everything up here was tidy. Totally neat and tidy. Almost pristine. I remember hearing the wind rubbing across the roof tiles and a quiet rattle somewhere. A child laughed down on the street.

Half the gable was lined. With red cloth and silver foil. There were a couple pillows and a load of toys lying around. A rose in a vase. First I thought, this looks nice—I swear, how dumb can you get, how could I have thought that? But I only thought it until I caught sight of some other stuff: handcuffs hanging neatly down from the sloping roof. Next to them a couple candy-colored pacifiers. Jay walked over to a pile of fabric in one corner. He unfolded the stuff: children's clothes. Babydolls, miniskirts, a load of belts. And next to the foil-cloth area were two large lamps with giant shades made of matte silver foil.

The front part of the gable looked like a computer nerd's bedroom. A long desk with a laptop, extra-huge screen, cables.

Jay was still kneeling down by the pile of clothes. He held up a pink babydoll, staring at it.

Then I spotted the camera.

It was small, attached to a thin-legged tripod next to the nerd desk, so I hadn't noticed it right away. I walked over and switched it on. I broke out in a total sweat, like I knew what I couldn't have known yet. I pressed Reverse. Kittiwake appeared on the display. She was wearing the babydoll. It had slid up her legs. No. It was hitched up with a belt. I pressed Reverse again, and again and again. Professor Bigshot and Kittiwake. Kittiwake and Professor Bigshot.

I kept pressing and pressing.

Then I went cold. Cold like never before. There was snow in my bones, ice. There was winter inside me. Something in my head turned to the left, then the right, back, forward, I swayed. I leaned hard on the tabletop. Then I puked right across the keyboard. I barfed over the cables, over everything. I puked and gagged. I gagged until nothing else came up except bitter green stuff.

* * *

No idea how long I sat there with Jay next to me, next to all the puke and the toys and next to the camera. I guess we were switched off. Right off. No feelings, just outer shell, skin—I wasn't cold anymore. There was nothing in me to be cold anymore, nothing there, we weren't there, we just weren't there. We couldn't be there. If we'd been there, we'd never have been alive. We'd never have been able to get up and leave. We weren't there anymore. All that stuff around us wasn't there.

There was nothing there.

When my telephone started vibrating I didn't understand what was going on, not for a long time. It was like a distant knocking, and you try to insert it into your dream so there's one thing you don't have to do: wake up. But it kept on and on.

Jay nudged me.

I took out my phone.

"Yes?"

"Dipper? It's me, Kite. Listen, I'm real worried. Kittiwake hasn't come home to my place. And it's been dark for hours now."

"What time is it?" I asked, and that was hard work.

I wiped a hand across my mouth, noticing it was still covered in puke.

"Nearly eight."

It was pitch black outside. I could see ice flowers on the slanting window above our heads. They were beautiful. And there were so many of them. The whole window was covered in these tiny white stars of frost. I thought, whoever came up with that? Ice flowers.

"Dipper? You still there?"

"Yeah."

"Is Jay with you?"

"Yeah."

"Can we go look for her together?"

I looked at Jay. He was sitting next to me, his head hanging down from his neck like a wet ball. I shook him by the shoulder.

"Jay, listen, Kittiwake's gone missing. We gotta find her."

Jay nodded. Real slowly.

"OK," I said into my phone. "We'll meet you outside the ladies' restrooms at the Mercado in twenty minutes. Maybe Kittiwake's just gone to visit my ma."

"See you there." Kite hung up.

We struggled to our feet.

Jay didn't say anything. He didn't do anything either. Just stood there.

I went over to the camera and took out the memory drive.

As we closed the trap door behind us, I thought:

Ice flowers. You wanna try those sometime.

ICE FLOES

Ma's workmate Olga was standing by the plate for her tips. She fetched an apple out of a paper bag and bit into it with a crunch. Jay and I were sitting on the leather bench in the restroom lobby.

"Your friend very pale." Olga gestured at Jay with her chin, chewing. "Shall I get Coke?"

I nodded.

Then she vanished, reappearing a minute later with a mini-bottle of soda. She handed me a cigarette lighter to open the cap. It was like Grand Central Station all round us. Coins clinking, doors slamming.

I levered the cap off the bottle and held it out to Jay. He hadn't said a word since the attic. Not looking at me, he took the bottle and drank. Then he handed it back and I emptied it in one gulp.

"I have new method." Olga threw the apple core in the designer trashcan. "You have to look people's eyes, or they not pay."

She stared at the next restroom visitor and smiled. He placed a coin on Olga's plate as he passed.

I thought of ice flowers.

Ma came jetting round the corner, and stopped short when she saw Jay and me sitting there.

"Hey, Ma," I said.

"Something happened?" she asked, depositing her cloth in her apron pocket.

"Friend very pale," Olga noted again.

I pulled myself together and managed a crooked smile. "Listen, has Kittiwake been here today?"

"When?" Ma eyed me like a bird of prey.

"You know, just now or whatever."

She snorted.

"You're telling me," she said, pretty mad. "And no kidding—I'm calling her mother when I've finished my shift, even if it's after ten! I'm not gonna stand by and watch the way that kid's running around anymore! It's freezing cold outside! It's not normal the way that kid dresses!"

Kite came down the hall.

Quickly, I stood up and walked toward her. I didn't want her to get anyone in a panic.

Behind me, I heard Jay ask, "So when was she here?"

"Don't know. Maybe an hour ago. But she only stayed a minute. I sent her home. It's too risky if they catch her here with us again."

"She was here an hour ago," I told Kite quietly.

"Did she say where she was going?" she whispered.

Kite was pale as death around the eyes. Drops of sweat glistened on her top lip. She must have been running.

I turned around.

"Did Kittiwake say where she was going, Ma?"

Ma flipped the designer trashcan open and took out the full bag. "I told you, I sent her home. She kept saying she'd told tales or something like that. I didn't quite get it, cause all hell's loose here today. Yeah, that was it though: telling tales, I think that's what she said." She took the trash bag to the corridor behind the ladies' room. "Kids, I've gotta work here! You can see what it's like today. I'm not done for an hour yet!"

Coins clinked, doors slammed. A woman inspected her teeth in a pocket mirror.

"Dry crackers!" Olga called after us. "And grated apple for stomach!"

"I think I know where she might be," I said on the escalator. "And I think we'd better get there quick."

* * *

When I think back to what happened next, I see the whole thing in slow motion without sound—or maybe with sound, but then everything sounds like it's underwater.

We ran halfway across town, taking all the hurdles, not making one diversion. The goal was the park. We kept on between the bare trees. I'd called Skylark, who came shooting out at us from one side and asked breathlessly:

"Man, what's up here anyway? It's below freezing and dark as night, comrades!"

"Kittiwake," was all I said, and I pointed at the river and a yellow buoy in the lamplight appearing at that moment. A sign swayed on the buoy:

"Beware of the weir, keep right!"

Sky didn't ask any more questions.

We all came to a stop on the little bridge leading to the other side of the park, from where you could see part of the weir. It was so quiet.

Ice floes were drifting on the river, like floating clouds or water lilies made of ice, just without the flowers. They made a faint scraping noise along the banks.

"You think she's here?" Kite looked at me.

Man, even now, even when my whole body and everything was totally focused on something else, I loved her. Yeah, that was it. I loved her, right here where we cast shadows in the lamplight.

"C'mon, guys!" I said, and we ran down off the bridge, along the river, until the roaring got louder and louder.

The ice floes jostled together. They were bobbing like crazy toward the weir. As if they were being steered by remote control, not knowing what awaited them.

The weir bridge. The lamplight.

The roaring and rushing of this water, crashing down several yards with full power. I bent over the wall, just like I had done an eternity ago with Kittiwake. Jay, Skylark, and Kite did the same. At the spot where the water sped downward hung a mess of branches that had somehow clasped themselves on there. Icicles and ice crystals stuck to them. The water must have been so damn cold you'd freeze to death if you hadn't already drowned.

"No!" Kite slapped her hands to her mouth. Her eyes were wide open. We followed her gaze.

On the wall behind the right weir tower, at least ten yards away from us, someone was facing the river. Standing pretty damn close to the edge. For a couple seconds, I couldn't do anything but stare at the figure's feet. Their toes were extended over the sheer drop. The water underneath looked calm, still as hell, and then all the ice floes crowding and pushing up against each other like children waiting for a treat. The waterfall was right between us and the figure, crazy loud.

We all stood there like we were frozen, staring across the weir. Than I pulled myself together. I signaled that no one should call out. If anyone shouted anything it'd be all over, I thought. Then Corone would fall or jump.

WHITE AS SNOW

I didn't want Jay to do a saut de détente over the weir—he was totally spaced out. I gave him my phone and told him in a whisper to call an ambulance. Then I looked over at Corone. He was staring down at the water, his torso swaying to and fro real strangely. We had no time to lose.

I swear it's completely different doing jumps in the park or at a play area or whatever, than if you're doing them where all hell's let loose below your feet. You're scared, more scared than you've ever been before, but you don't have time to start whining and weeping. Because on the other side is a guy standing there like he's on the edge of a cliff, and what happens next is all down to you. I guess Skylark and Kite felt it like I did. Our advantage was that the weir was so damn loud that Corone probably couldn't hear us approaching.

From the bridge, we jumped one after another onto a platform next to the tower. There was a huge drop right behind it. I guessed the distance to the next wall was about twelve feet. We didn't have much space to take a run-up. Skylark signaled to us. Kite looked at me. I didn't want her to jump, but I realized I wouldn't be able to stop her. And I knew she was a traceuse.

Not needing any explanations, the three of us focused on our goal: the opposite wall. Then we took two steps and jumped. We jumped over the raging canyon. We grabbed hold of the edge of that wall. For a fraction of a second, I registered that we'd made the leap, and then I noticed I was slipping. There was a layer of ice beneath my hands. I was losing control. Below me roared the waterfall, the cold of its ice water rising up to meet me like ghostly fingers. I looked over at Kite and saw she was struggling, just like me. Man, I thought, it's all over for us. Love or not, time's up. I clawed my fingers into the bricks, but I couldn't get a grip.

Then something came over me. I don't know exactly what, maybe like a lever in my head flicking over to the other side. Give it up with the damn loser shit! said something inside my half-frozen brain. It's only ice for God's sake.

And all of a sudden I found the strength, like someone somewhere had poured it over me and inside of me.

With only my fingertips on the slippery edge of the wall, I pulled myself up slowly. Inch by inch. I focused all the power I had on my eight fingertips on the edge of that wall. My upper arms were as tensed as you can get. Then, finally, I levered myself up onto the platform.

Kite and Skylark made it up at the same moment as me.

Corone was now about twenty feet away from us.

We hadn't taken two steps in his direction when something screamed like crazy. A giant crow, the size of a damn dog. It swung up out of the tree by the weir tower, screeching and screeching.

Corone turned around. He turned around too damn fast. Then he slipped on the fucking icy ground of the weir.

Everything went so fast that I can't remember it exactly. One of us did a roulade toward Corone. Someone balanced across the ice like it was a narrow rail. One of us took two huge leaps. I don't know which one was me, which was Sky-lark and Kite. We were like parts of a single person. It took one second, and Corone had six hands on his body. And that was damn lucky for him, 'cause he happened to be dangling over that ice-cold water.

We dragged at Corone's jacket, his hood, his pants, everything we got our hands on.

I couldn't think normal thoughts again until he was lying on the platform in front of us.

He was breathing like hell.

His face was white as snow.

* * *

Once the ambulance had taken Corone away, we walked back through the park in silence. Someone passed us on a bike, the rear light shining red, as rear lights tend to do, and I thought it was completely crazy, now that nothing in the world was normal. Nothing was normal. I read a tag on a wall: RADICALS, and when we got to the street there was a gang of skinheads standing there yelling: "A German is a German!" over and over again.

"What about Kittiwake?" asked Kite.

"Come on." I gestured to my friends to follow me.

* * *

Ma was just hanging up the phone as we came in the kitchen.

"Where's her mother got to?" she cursed instead of a greeting. "I've been trying to reach her for two hours. And it's after eleven! The kid's asleep in my bed. Says she'd rather live here. I'm about to explode, no kiddin'!"

We exchanged glances. I think I could hear the weight falling from the Urbans' shoulders like stones on the kitchen floor.

"Ma," I said, sitting down at the table.

Skylark, Jay, and Kite joined me.

"Will you make us a coffee? There's something we have to tell you."

FLOWERS AND DUST

Telling my ma the whole story was pretty bad. She'd been through enough shit, I thought. And now this. But she was pretty cool, once she'd cried and all that. She said we had to go to the police first thing in the morning about Professor Bigshot, so they could arrest him and whatever.

Jay—boy, I don't know, he was the real poor bastard in the whole thing. He sat there at the table like a defendant in a courtroom. His father was a dirty perverted child abuser and made films of it—I mean, how are you supposed to deal with that? We heard a hell of a lot of real bad things about the whole thing, once we'd told the cops and given them the memory stick and once they'd woken Professor Bigshot at four in the morning and confiscated everything on his hard drive. I swear he tried to run off out the back door, but they'd posted a couple cops in the backyard. That sick bastard. He even told them Kittiwake had enjoyed it, that it was like putting on a play at the dipshit school for her and she couldn't get enough of it. He said they ought to "relax" the laws because children like sex so much. Every time I think of him and the pictures on that camera, I feel like puking again. I have to take deep breaths every time so the nausea goes away. Sometimes I go to the restroom paradise if it won't stop and drink a Coke with Olga. But I guess you can't sit around there all day, on the waiting bench.

Professor Bigshot got four years for child abuse and the child pornos. By the time he comes out, Kittiwake'll be four-teen. Then she'll be too old for his taste, but there'll be other girls. I'm so damn mad at the guy, I can't guarantee for anything if I met him in a dark alley. I swear. But sure, the guy's clever and all that, he'll move somewhere else and start over.

Kittiwake's in a children's home now. It's not too bad there; Ma and I visited her. Nice people and whatever. Hot food, proper clothes, and she shares a room with another girl. She goes to a shrink twice a week, and she's supposed to help her deal with all the shit and stuff.

They put Corone in a residential group for teenagers. I don't think it's all that great there, but I mean, they have water and electricity and he has a room of his own. Better than before. And by the way: he didn't know anything about the thing with Professor Bigshot and Kittiwake—he just wanted to scare the bastard that evening. Yeah. You wouldn't believe how relieved I was to find that out. I have to admit I really thought for a while that he'd known about the whole thing and not protected Kittiwake. When Corone heard what had really been going on, he said he'd be better off drowned. It still gets to him, even though he acts like every-thing's fine with him. I can tell. The guy's my friend, after all.

His mother got done for neglect. The guy she'd been with the whole time was the least nice man she'd ever had in her life, or that's what Corone says. But she still stayed with him. I don't know—how's anyone supposed to understand all this shit?

Kite and Corone are sometimes together, sometimes not—don't ask me. Corone still doesn't know to this day, I guess, that she was a traceuse long before the Urbans. I've stopped being Kite's shoulder to cry on. But I still think she's pretty damn cool, even though I don't wanna kiss her and all that. That's just a fact. She's saving for a flight to Vancouver and now she has space in her apartment again to fold her paper animals and whatever. I guess she's gonna be pretty good some day. She's pretty good at everything actually: math, pepper hot chocolate, origami, parkour. It took me quite a while to deal with the fact that we're never gonna be an item. But I guess I did enough fighting for her. Or with myself.

Then we did something else: we made an awesome video of our parkour skills. It's on the net now—last time I looked it had 3467 views and five stars. Sky had a fish-eye for special effects. He edited the video real cool, and he insisted on using Museum's "Flowers and Dust" as the backing and not some hip-hop track that Corone wanted.

Yeah, and then there's Jay.

He's gone. Had to make a hell of a lotta statements in court, and I guess that was too much for him. He was eighteen, he could do what he wanted. We didn't know where he was for months, until we got a card from him. From Canada. He's living there with his mother and his brother, the perfect one. Maybe we'll all go visit him some time, if we have the money.

And me?

First I had to make up for punching my workmate in the face. Community service, plus a fine. And now I'm thinking about going back to school. No kidding. Not exactly to learn about those two Japanese paper-folders' Huzita-Hatori axioms or whatever, but because I wanna get off the construction sites.

Corone and me wanna hitchhike to France next summer—to Lisses, the birthplace of parkour. You meet a whole load of traceurs there. I'm looking forward to it like crazy already.

And I'll tell you something else.

A couple weeks after all the horror, once the spring had settled into the trees and everything and it was getting warmer, this girl suddenly showed up at our training session.

And me and her are hanging out now.

Extra-terrestrial and all that.

Totally gorgeous.

I don't know if all this is a story now.

I'm just not that kinda guy.

Mercy.

But keep on moving!

Cheers!

Your Dipper.

APPENDIX: BASIC PARKOUR MOVES

Atterrissage or réception: landing on your feet, usually supporting your upper body with your hands

Équilibre: balancing on walls or poles; trains your sense of equilibrium

Franchissement: swinging through a gap (for example two horizontal poles)

Lâché: dropping from a hanging position, possibly to swing onto another object

Passe muraille: crossing a wall by pushing off from it, transforming forward motion into a vertical movement

Passement: generally overcoming an obstacle

Demi-tour: a 180-degree turn over an obstacle, with a controlled landing afterward

Révers: a 360-degree turn over an obstacle with a controlled landing; this move is often used to gain speed from the centrifugal force it creates for further moves

Planche: transfer from a hanging position to a braced position; you can work with either momentum or strength, or combine the two

Roulade: a roll transforming vertical energy into a forward movement; your knees should not be bent at more than 90 degrees; you roll at a slant across your back and not along your spine

Saut de bras: jumping onto an object and landing in a hanging position; your legs should touch the object first to brake the impact; then you pull yourself up the object using your arms (see: Planche)

Saut de chat: a squat jump off an object with your legs drawn in; the higher the obstacle, the lower you have to bend before the jump to gain height

Saut de fond: all jumps from a raised surface to the ground; depending on the height and the forward motion, you might want to take a roll afterward

Saut de détente: a long jump from one object to another; this technique is used, for example, to overcome gaps or obstacles with a run-up

Saut de précision: a jump to a previously defined landing spot; the aim is to land in a standing position precisely on the right spot

Tic-tac: pushing off from an object (for example a wall), to overcome an unstable or small obstacle

ABOUT THE AUTHOR

Photo © Peter von Sághy

Rusalka Reh was born in Melbourne, Australia, in 1970 and grew up in Germany. She studied special education, rehabilitation, and art therapy in Cologne. She began her career as a scientific assistant at the university's fine arts program and later worked as an art therapist in municipal children's homes. Since 2000, she has been working as a freelance author, writing lyrics and prose and, in addition to books for children and adults, she has published several texts in anthologies and magazines.

ABOUT THE TRANSLATOR

Katy Derbyshire is a London-born translator based in Berlin. She has translated various contemporary German writers including Clemens Meyer, Inka Parei, and Helene Hegemann, and co-edited a book of writing on her new home, *City-Lit Berlin*.